GETTING IT ON

A CONDOM READER

GETTING IT ON

A CONDOM READER

EDITED BY
MITCH ROBERSON AND JULIA DUBNER

Published by
Soho Press
853 Broadway
New York, New York 10003

Library of Congress Cataloging-in-Publication Data
Getting it on: a condom reader
edited by Mitch Roberson and Julia Dubner — 1st ed.
p.   cm.
ISBN: paperback 1-56947-125-8 (alk. paper)
hardcover 1-56947-145-2 (alk. paper)
1. Condoms–Literary collections. 2. American literature–20th century.
3. Birth control–Literary collections. 4. Sex–Literary collections.
I. Roberson, Mitch, 1966–   . II. Dubner, Julia, 1966–   .
PS509.C593G48 1999   98–3722
810.8 ' 03538–dc21   CIP

10 9 8 7 6 5 4 3 2 1

Getting It On is dedicated to Donna Rosenstiel and
Peter Megginson, without whom we would not have been able
to pull it off.

M.M.: ". . . it was Love who invented these little jackets, but he had to ally himself with Precaution; and it seems to me that the alliance must have been displeasing to him, for it belongs only to the dark realm of Policy."

Casanova: "Alas, that is true! You astound me. But, my dear friend, we will philosophize afterward."

—Giacomo Casanova, *History of My Life*

CONTENTS

ACKNOWLEDGMENTS

We would like to thank the following people for their encouragement, ideas, and practical help in putting this book together: Elizabeth Binggeli, John Buterbaugh, David Clewell, Lucinda Ebersole, Elizabeth Feinman, Marcia Hack, Ed Henley, David Jacobs, Richard Peabody, Lois Rosenthal, Sue Starkweather, Abigail Wender, Phyllis Wender, and all the other friends and colleagues who gave valuable input along the way. Thanks to our families for offering unconditional support. We appreciate the ongoing work of the magazines that originally published many of our selections: *Antaeus, Djinni, Georgia Review, Iowa Review, Kenyon Review, New England Review, New Republic, Playboy, Prairie Schooner, Story,* and *Witness*. Thanks to the following organizations, whose resources helped us tremendously in our research: Associated Writing Programs, District of Columbia Public Library, Jersey City Public Library, Library of Congress, New York Public Library, Poets and Writers, Poets House, and the Writer's Center.

Immeasurable thanks to our agent, Jill Grinberg, for taking this book on as a labor of love, and for her expertise, tenacity, insight, and constant enthusiasm and encouragement.

• In Memoriam •
William Matthews

INTRODUCTION

CONDOMS ARE EVERYWHERE—television shows, rap lyrics, class-rooms, not to mention bedrooms and back seats. They can be fla-vored, textured, colored, and even patriotic. Everybody has an anecdote about buying condoms, finding used condoms, fumbling for condoms in the dark. So why not a book?

Our process for selecting this book's contents consisted of both meticulous and serendipitous research. We read hundreds of poems, stories, and novel excerpts in books and literary maga-zines—looking for the dirty parts. We considered over 200 sub-missions from all over the country. Our main criterion was that condoms be thematically integral; a mere mention wouldn't do. What we found was an imaginative variety of poetry and prose.

T. Coraghessan Boyle takes the idea of caution in a new rela-tionship to a dark extreme. In a story that first appeared in the *San Francisco Chronicle* in the early 1980s—and was the first published fiction to address the AIDS epidemic—Armistead Maupin chron-icles the time when the disease was just beginning to affect gay men and everyone else. Martha Elizabeth finds a spark of absur-dity in all that "safety" entails.

Michelle Chalfoun writes of the harrowing circumstances that precede and follow a young circus worker's trip to buy condoms. William Matthews examines them as protection from "friendly fire" in the internal "civil war" of AIDS. John Irving portrays the innocent ignorance that is so often part of the common experi-ence of condoms.

Anne Rice shows us that condoms and vampires don't mix. In a string of excerpts from his novel *Praise*, Andrew McGahan explores the downside of self-destruction. Gregg Shapiro chroni-cles a gay man's journey from youthful experimentation to AIDS awareness, armed not only with latex, but also with a belief in the hopefulness of sexuality.

A portion of the proceeds from the sales of this book will go to the Condom Resource Center, sponsor of National Condom Week. This donation would not be possible without the generosity of many authors who chose to forgo payment and add their fees directly to our own contribution.

Getting It On. Our title speaks to the many chords we hope this book strikes. Getting it on is about sex. It is about getting on with life and relationships in the face of all the risks, both emotional and physical, that sexuality involves. And finally, getting it on is about a moment—not an abstract public health maxim nor a sanctimonious warning—but a moment of humility and humanity.

— Mitch Roberson and Julia Dubner
Jersey City, New Jersey

MODERN LOVE

T. Coraghessan Boyle

THERE WAS NO exchange of body fluids on the first date, and that suited both of us just fine. I picked her up at seven, took her to Mee Grop, where she meticulously separated each sliver of meat from her Phat Thai, watched her down four bottles of Singha at three dollars per, and then gently stroked her balsam-smelling hair while she snoozed through *The Terminator* at the Circle Shopping Center theater. We had a late-night drink at Rigoletto's Pizza Bar (and two slices, plain cheese), and I dropped her off. The moment we pulled up in front of her apartment she had the door open. She turned to me with the long, elegant, mournful face of her Puritan ancestors and held out her hand.

"It's been fun," she said.

"Yes," I said, taking her hand.

She was wearing gloves.

"I'll call you," she said.

"Good," I said, giving her my richest smile. "And I'll call you."

On the second date we got acquainted.

"I can't tell you what a strain it was for me the other night," she said, staring down into her chocolate-mocha-fudge sundae. It was early afternoon, we were in Helmut's Olde Tyme Ice Cream Parlor in Mamaroneck, and the sun streamed through the thick frosted windows and lit the place like a convalescent home. The fixtures glowed behind the counter, the brass rail was buffed to a reflec-

1

tive sheen, and everything smelled of disinfectant. We were the only people in the place.

"What do you mean?" I said, my mouth glutinous with melted marshmallow and caramel.

"I mean Thai food, the seats in the movie theater, the *ladies' room* in that place for god's sake . . ."

"Thai food?" I wasn't following her. I recalled the maneuver with the strips of pork and the fastidious dissection of the glass noodles. "You're a vegetarian?"

She looked away in exasperation, and then gave me the full, wide-eyed shock of her ice-blue eyes. "Have you seen the Health Department statistics on sanitary conditions in ethnic restaurants?"

I hadn't.

Her eyebrows leapt up. She was earnest. She was lecturing. "These people are refugees. They have—well, different standards. They haven't even been inoculated." I watched her dig the tiny spoon into the recesses of the dish and part her lips for a neat, foursquare morsel of ice cream and fudge.

"The illegals, anyway. And that's half of them." She swallowed with an almost imperceptible movement, a shudder, her throat dipping and rising like a gazelle's. "I got drunk from fear," she said. "Blind panic. I couldn't help thinking I'd wind up with hepatitis or dysentery or dengue fever or something."

"Dengue fever?"

"I usually bring a disposable sanitary sheet for public theaters— just think of who might have been in that seat before you, and how many times, and what sort of nasty festering little cultures of this and that there must be in all those ancient dribbles of taffy and Coke and extra-butter popcorn—but I didn't want you to think I was too extreme or anything on the first date, so I didn't. And then the *ladies' room* . . . You don't think I'm overreacting, do you?"

2

As a matter of fact, I did. Of course I did. I liked Thai food—and sushi and ginger crab and greasy souvlaki at the corner stand too. There was the look of the mad saint in her eye, the obsessive, the mortifier of the flesh, but I didn't care. She was lovely, wilting, clear-eyed, and pure, as cool and matchless as if she'd stepped out of a Pre-Raphaelite painting, and I was in love. Besides, I tended a little that way myself. Hypochondria. Anal retentiveness. The ordered environment and alphabetized books. I was a thirty-three-year-old bachelor, I carried some scars and I read the news-papers—herpes, AIDS, the Asian clap that foiled every antibiotic in the book. I was willing to take it slow. "No," I said, "I don't think you're overreacting at all."

I paused to draw in a breath so deep it might have been a sigh. "I'm sorry," I whispered, giving her a dog like look of contrition. "I didn't know."

She reached out then and touched my hand—touched it, skin to skin—and murmured that it was all right, she'd been through worse. "If you want to know," she breathed, "I like places like this."

I glanced around. The place was still empty, but for Helmut, in a blinding white jumpsuit and toque, studiously polishing the tile walls. "I know what you mean," I said.

We dated for a month—museums, drives in the country, French and German restaurants, ice-cream emporia, fern bars—before we kissed. And when we kissed, after a showing of *David and Lisa* at a revival house all the way up in Rhinebeck and on a night so cold no run-of-the-mill bacterium or commonplace virus could have survived it, it was the merest brushing of the lips. She was wear-ing a big-shouldered coat of synthetic fur and a knit hat pulled down over her brow and she hugged my arm as we stepped out of the theater and into the blast of the night. "God," she said, "did you see him when he screamed 'You touched me!'? Wasn't that priceless?" Her eyes were big and she seemed weirdly excited. "Sure," I said, "yeah, it was great," and then she pulled me close and kissed me. I felt the soft flicker of her lips against mine. "I love you," she said, "I think."

A month of dating and one dry fluttering kiss. At this point you might begin to wonder about me, but really, I didn't mind. As I say, I was willing to wait—I had the patience of Sisyphus—and it was enough just to be with her. Why rush things? I thought. This is good, this is charming, like the slow sweet unfolding of the romance in a Frank Capra movie, where sweetness and light always prevail. Sure, she had her idiosyncrasies, but who didn't? Frankly, I'd never been comfortable with the three-drinks-dinner-and-bed sort of thing, the girls who come on like they've been in prison for six years and just got out in time to put on their make-up and jump into the passenger seat of your car. Breda—that was her name, Breda Drumhill, and the very sound and syllabification of it made me melt—was different.

Finally, two weeks after the trek to Rhinebeck, she invited me to her apartment. Cocktails, she said. Dinner. A quiet evening in front of the tube.

She lived in Croton, on the ground floor of a restored Victorian, half a mile from the Harmon station, where she caught the train each morning for Manhattan and her job as an editor of *Anthropology Today*. She'd held the job since graduating from Barnard six years earlier (with a double major in Rhetoric and Alien Cultures), and it suited her temperament perfectly. Field anthropologists living among the River Dayak of Borneo or the Kurds of Kurdistan would send her rough and grammatically tortured accounts of their observations and she would whip them into shape for popular consumption. Naturally, filth and exotic disease, as well as outlandish customs and revolting habits, played a leading role in her rewrites. Every other day or so she'd call me from work and in a voice that could barely contain its joy give me the details of some new and horrific disease she'd discovered.

She met me at the door in a silk kimono that featured a plunging neckline and a pair of dragons with intertwined tails. Her hair was pinned up as if she'd just stepped out of the bath and she smelled of Noxzema and pHisoHex. She pecked my cheek, took the bottle of Vouvray I held out in offering, and led me into the front room. "Chagas' disease," she said, grinning wide to show off her perfect, outsized teeth.

"Chagas' disease?" I echoed, not quite knowing what to do with myself. The room was as spare as a monk's cell. Two chairs, a loveseat, and a coffee table, in glass, chrome, and hard black plastic. No plants ("God knows what sort of insects might live on them—and the *dirt*, the dirt has got to be crawling with bacteria, not to mention spiders and worms and things") and no rug ("A breeding ground for fleas and ticks and chiggers").

Still grinning, she steered me to the hard black plastic loveseat and sat down beside me, the Vouvray cradled in her lap. "South America," she whispered, her eyes leaping with excitement. "In the jungle. These bugs—assassin bugs, they're called—isn't that wild? These bugs bite you and then, after they've sucked on you awhile, they go potty next to the wound. When you scratch, it gets into your bloodstream, and anywhere from one to twenty years later you get a disease that's like a cross between malaria and AIDS."

"And then you die," I said.

"And then you die."

Her voice had turned somber. She wasn't grinning any longer. What could I say? I patted her hand and flashed a smile. "Yum," I said, mugging for her. "What's for dinner?"

She served a cold cream-of-tofu-carrot soup and little lentil-

paste sandwiches for an appetizer and a garlic souffle with bio-
logically controlled vegetables for the entrée. Then it was snifters
of cognac, the big-screen TV, and a movie called *The Boy in the
Bubble*, about a kid raised in a totally antiseptic environment
because he was born without an immune system. No one could
touch him. Even the slightest sneeze would have killed him. Breda
sniffled through the first half-hour, then pressed my hand and
sobbed openly as the boy finally crawled out of the bubble,
caught about thirty-seven different diseases, and died before the
commercial break. "I've seen this movie six times now," she said,
fighting to control her voice, "and it gets to me every time. What
a life," she said, waving her snifter at the screen, "what a perfect
life. Don't you envy him?"

I didn't envy him. I envied the jade pendant that dangled
between her breasts and I told her so.

She might have giggled or gasped or lowered her eyes, but she
didn't. She gave me a long slow look, as if she were deciding
something, and then she allowed herself to blush, the color suf-
fusing her throat in a delicious mottle of pink and white. "Give me
a minute," she said mysteriously, and disappeared into the bathroom.

I was electrified. This was it. Finally. After all the avowals, the
pressed hands, the little jokes and routines, after all the miles driv-
en, meals consumed, museums paced, and movies watched, we
were finally, naturally, gracefully going to come together in the
ultimate act of intimacy and love.

I felt hot. There were beads of sweat on my forehead. I didn't
know whether to stand or sit. And then the lights dimmed, and
there she was at the rheostat.

She was still in her kimono, but her hair was pinned up more
severely, wound in a tight coil to the crown of her head, as if she'd
girded herself for battle. And she held something in her hand—a

slim package, wrapped in plastic. It rustled as she crossed the room.

"When you're in love, you make love," she said, easing down beside me on the rocklike settee, "—it's only natural." She handed me the package. "I don't want to give you the wrong impression," she said, her voice throaty and raw, "just because I'm careful and modest and because there's so much, well, filth in the world, but I have my passionate side too. I do. And I love you. I think"

"Yes," I said, groping for her, the package all but forgotten.

We kissed. I rubbed the back of her neck, felt something strange, an odd sag and ripple, as if her skin had suddenly turned to Saran Wrap, and then she had her hand on my chest. "Wait," she breathed, "the, the thing."

I sat up. "Thing?"

The light was dim but I could see the blush invade her face now. She was sweet. Oh, she was sweet, my Little Em'ly, my Victorian princess. "It's Swedish," she said.

I looked down at the package in my lap. It was a clear, skinlike sheet of plastic, folded up in its transparent package like a heavy-duty garbage bag. I held it up to her huge, trembling eyes. A crazy idea darted in and out of my head. No, I thought.

"It's the newest thing," she said, the words coming in a rush, "the safest . . . I mean, nothing could possibly—"

My face was hot. "No," I said.

"It's a condom," she said, tears starting up in her eyes, "my doctor got them for me they're . . . they're Swedish." Her face wrinkled up and she began to cry. "It's a condom," she sobbed, crying so hard the kimono fell open and I could see the outline of the thing against the swell of her nipples, "a full-body condom."

I was offended. I admit it. It wasn't so much her obsession with germs and contagion, but that she didn't trust me after all that

7

time. I was clean. Quintessentially clean. I was a man of moderate habits and good health, I changed my underwear and socks daily—sometimes twice a day—and I worked in an office, with clean, crisp, unequivocal numbers, managing my late father's chain of shoe stores (and he died cleanly himself, of a myocardial infarction, at seventy-five). "But Breda," I said, reaching out to console her and brushing her soft, plastic-clad breast in the process, "don't you trust me? Don't you believe in me? Don't you, don't you love me?" I took her by the shoulders, lifted her head, forced her to look me in the eye. "I'm clean," I said. "Trust me."

She looked away. "Do it for me," she said in her smallest voice, "if you really love me."

In the end, I did it. I looked at her, crying, crying for me, and I looked at the thin sheet of plastic clinging to her, and I did it. She helped me into the thing, poked two holes for my nostrils, zipped the plastic zipper up the back, and pulled it tight over my head. It fit like a wetsuit. And the whole thing—the stroking and the tenderness and the gentle yielding—was everything I'd hoped it would be.

Almost.

She called me from work the next day. I was playing with sales figures and thinking of her. "Hello," I said, practically cooing into the receiver.

"You've got to hear this." Her voice was giddy with excitement.

"Hey," I said, cutting her off in a passionate whisper, "last night was really special."

"Oh, yes," she said, "yes, last night. It was. And I love you, I. . . do." She paused to draw in her breath. "But listen to this: I just got a piece from a man and his wife living among the Tuareg of Nigeria—these are the people who follow cattle around, picking up the dung for their cooking fires?"

I made a small noise of awareness.

"Well, they make their huts of dung too—isn't that wild? And guess what—when times are hard, when the crops fail and the cattle can barely stand up, you know what they eat?"

"Let me guess," I said. "Dung?"

She let out a whoop. "Yes! Yes! Isn't it too much? They *eat* dung!"

I'd been saving one for her, a disease a doctor friend had told me about. "Onchocerciasis," I said. "You know it?"

There was a thrill in her voice. "Tell me."

"South America and Africa both. A fly bites you and lays its eggs in your bloodstream and when the eggs hatch, the larvae— these little white worms—migrate to your eyeballs, right underneath the membrane there, so you can see them wriggling around."

There was a silence on the other end of the line.

"Breda?"

"That's sick," she said. "That's really sick."

But I thought—? I trailed off. "Sorry," I said.

"Listen," and the edge came back into her voice, "the reason I called is because I love you, I think I love you, and I want you to meet somebody."

"Sure," I said.

"I want you to meet Michael. Michael Maloney."

"Sure. Who's he?"

She hesitated, paused just a beat, as if she knew she was going too far. "My doctor," she said.

You have to work at love. You have to bend, make subtle adjustments, sacrifices—love is nothing without sacrifice. I went to Dr. Maloney. Why not? I'd eaten tofu, bantered about leprosy and bilharziasis as if I were immune, and made love in a bag. If it made Breda happy—if it eased the nagging fears that ate at her day and night—then it was worth it.

The doctor's office was in Scarsdale, in his home, a two-tone mock Tudor with a winding drive and oaks as old as my grandfather's Chrysler. He was a young man—late thirties, I guessed—with a red beard, shaved head, and a pair of oversized spectacles in clear plastic frames. He took me right away—the very day I called—and met me at the door himself. "Breda's told me about you," he said, leading me into the floodlit vault of his office. He looked at me appraisingly a moment, murmuring "Yes, yes" into his beard, and then, with the aid of his nurses, Miss Archibald and Miss Slivovitz, put me through a battery of tests that would have embarrassed an astronaut.

First, there were the measurements, including digital joints, maxilla, cranium, penis, and earlobe. Next the rectal exam, the EEG and urine sample. And then the tests. Stress tests, patch tests, reflex tests, lung-capacity tests (I blew up yellow balloons till they popped, then breathed into a machine the size of a Hammond organ), the X-rays, sperm count, and a closely printed, twenty-four-page questionnaire that included sections on dream analysis, genealogy, and logic and reasoning. He drew blood too, of course—to test vital-organ function and exposure to disease. "We're testing for antibodies to over fifty diseases," he said, eyes dodging behind the walls of his lenses. "You'd be surprised how many people have been infected without even knowing it." I couldn't tell if he was joking or not. On the way out he took my arm and told me he'd have the results in a week.

That week was the happiest of my life. I was with Breda every night, and over the weekend we drove up to Vermont to stay at a hygiene center her cousin had told her about. We dined by candlelight—on real food—and afterward we donned the Saran Wrap suits and made joyous, sanitary love. I wanted more, of course—the touch of skin on skin—but I was fulfilled and I was happy. Go slow, I told myself. All things in time. One night, as we lay entwined in the big white fortress of her bed, I stripped back the hood of the plastic suit and asked her if she'd ever trust me enough to make love in the way of the centuries, raw and unprotected. She twisted free of her own wrapping and looked away, giving me that matchless patrician profile. "Yes," she said, her voice pitched low, "yes, of course. Once the results are in."

"Results?"

She turned to me, her eyes searching mine. "Don't tell me you've forgotten?"

I had. Carried away, intense, passionate, brimming with love, I'd forgotten.

"Silly you," she murmured, tracing the line of my lips with a slim, plastic-clad finger. "Does the name Michael Maloney ring a bell?"

And then the roof fell in.

I called and there was no answer. I tried her at work and her secretary said she was out. I left messages. She never called back. It was as if we'd never known one another, as if I were a stranger, a door-to-door salesman, a beggar on the street.

I took up a vigil in front of her house. For a solid week I sat in my parked car and watched the door with all the fanatic devotion of a pilgrim at a shrine. Nothing. She neither came nor went. I rang the phone off the hook, interrogated her friends, haunted the elevator, the hallway, and the reception room at her office. She'd disappeared.

Finally, in desperation, I called her cousin in Larchmont. I'd met her once—she was a homely, droopy-sweatered, baleful-looking girl who represented everything gone wrong in the genes that had come to such glorious fruition in Breda—and barely knew what to say to her. I'd made up a speech, something about how my mother was dying in Phoenix, the business was on the rocks, I was drinking too much and dwelling on thoughts of suicide, destruction, and final judgment, and I had to talk to Breda just one more time before the end, and did she by any chance know where she was? As it turned out, I didn't need the speech. Breda answered the phone.

"Breda, it's me," I choked. "I've been going crazy looking for you."

Silence.

"Breda, what's wrong? Didn't you get my messages?"

Her voice was halting, distant. "I can't see you anymore," she said.

"Can't see me?" I was stunned, hurt, angry. "What do you mean?"

"All those feet," she said.

"Feet?" It took me a minute to realize she was talking about the shoe business. "But I don't deal with anybody's feet—I work in an office. Like you. With air-conditioning and sealed windows. I haven't touched a foot since I was sixteen."

"Athlete's foot," she said. "Psoriasis. Eczema. Jungle rot."

"What is it? The physical?" My voice cracked with outrage. "Did I flunk the damn physical? Is that it?"

She wouldn't answer me.

A chill went through me. "What did he say? What did the son of a bitch say?"

There was a distant ticking over the line, the pulse of time and space, the gentle sway of Bell Telephone's hundred million miles of wire.

"Listen," I pleaded, "see me one more time, just once—that's all I ask. We'll talk it over. We could go on a picnic. In the park. We could spread a blanket and, and we could sit on opposite corners—"

12

"Lyme disease," she said.

"Lyme disease?"

"Spread by tick bite. They're seething in the grass. You get Bell's palsy, meningitis, the lining of your brain swells up like dough."

"Rockefeller Center then," I said. "By the fountain."

Her voice was dead. "Pigeons," she said. "They're like flying rats."

"Helmut's. We can meet at Helmut's. Please. I love you."

"I'm sorry."

"Breda, please listen to me. We were so close—"

"Yes," she said, "we were close," and I thought of that first night in her apartment, the boy in the bubble and the Saran Wrap suit, thought of the whole dizzy spectacle of our romance till her voice came down like a hammer on the refrain, "but not that close."

ALL THAT TALK ABOUT 'HIGH-TECH' IN THE FUTURE NOTWITHSTANDING, WHY THE 21ST CENTURY MIGHT WELL TURN OUT TO BE FULL OF A WHOLE LOT OF CLUMSY PEOPLE!

Michael Benedikt

A great many people who are clumsy
                              will exist, almost certainly,
                                                  in the 21st century
That will be because
                        their forebears
                                      reproduced disproportionately,
Due to their inability
                        to tear the little tinfoil covers
                                              off condoms properly
—Thus, ripping their rubbers in the process!

Oh, graceful children!
  you will have to learn to live with them (all those clumsy ones!)
& When you step outside your doors
Perhaps wear plastic
                    shoulderguards
                              & hockey shin-guards
                                          & even crash helmets
                                          & maybe metal-toed shoes
Because the heirs of all those clumsy people
                    will keep on running straight into you on the street

— & Learn to properly utilize earplugs, too,
Because of the sounds of things crashing to the ground incessantly

                        from being
                                  dropped
                                        or fall-
                                              ing
                                                      ve
                                                        r
                                                    o

Excerpt from BABYCAKES: CAMPMATES

Armistead Maupin

As DAWN CREPT over Death Valley, Michael stirred in his sleeping bag and catalogued the sounds of the desert: the twitter of tiny birds, the frantic scampering of kangaroo rats, the soothing rustle of the wind in the mesquite trees . . .

"Oh, no! The vinaigrette leaked!"

. . . the voice of Scotty, their chef for this expedition, taking stock of his inventory in preparation for breakfast. His plight provoked a burst of laughter from Ned's tent, followed by more of the same from the sandy bluff where Roger and Gary had slept under the stars.

"What's so fucking funny?" yelled Scotty.

Ned answered: "That's the nelliest thing that's ever been said in Death Valley."

"If you want butch," the chef snapped, "try the third RV on the right—they're eating Spam and powdered eggs. Us nellie numbers will be having eggs benedict, thank you."

General cheers all around.

A tent was unzipped, probably Douglas and Paul's. Boots crunched against gravel, then came Paul's voice, froggy with sleep. "Does anybody know the way to the bathroom?"

More laughter from Ned. "You didn't really believe that, did you?"

"Listen, dickhead, you told me there was running water."

Roger came to the rescue. "All the way down the road, on the right-hand side."

"Where's my shaving kit?" asked Paul.

"Behind the ice chest," said Douglas.

Turtle-like, Michael inched out of his sleeping bag, found the air decidedly nippy, and popped back in again. There was no point in being rash about this. His absence from the banter had not yet been observed. He could still grab some sleep.

Wrong. Scotty's smiling face was now framed in the window of his tent. "Good morning, bright eyes."

Michael emerged part of the way and gave him a sleepy salute.

"Are you heading for the bathroom?" the chef asked.

"Eventually."

"Good. Find me some *garni*, would you?"

"Uh . . . *garni*?"

"For the grapefruit," explained Scotty. "There's lots of nice stuff along the road."

"Right."

"Just something pretty. It doesn't have to be edible, of course."

"Of course."

Garni in Death Valley. There was bound to be a message there somewhere—about life and irony and the gay sensibility—but it eluded him completely as he stood at a sink in the middle of nowhere and brushed his teeth next to a fat man in Bermuda shorts and flip-flops.

On the way back to the campsite, he left the path long enough to find something suitably decorative—a lacy, pale-green weed that didn't appear to shed—then decided on an alternate return route. He felt strangely exhilarated by the brisk, blue morning, and he wanted to enjoy the sensation in solitude.

They had pitched their tents along the edge of a dry creekbed at the northern end of the Mesquite Springs campground, where a kindly quirk of geography kept the neighboring RVs out of sight behind a rocky rise. As a consequence, he had trouble finding the

campsite until he spotted the sand-colored gables of the Big Tent—
a free-form communal space Ned had built with bamboo poles and
tarps from the nursery.

Breakfast was a success. Scotty's eggs benedict were a triumph,
and Michael's *garni* received a polite round of applause. When the
table had been cleared, Douglas and Paul began heating water for
dishwashing, while Roger and Gary repaired to their corner to
divide the mushrooms into seven equal portions. After each had
downed his share, Ned proposed a hike into the Last Chance
Mountains. "I have something to show you." he told Michael in
private. "Something special."

Scotty stayed behind to fix lunch while everybody else followed Ned into the hills, stopping sporadically to exclaim over a
flowering cactus or an exotic rock formation. (Douglas was positive he had seen hieroglyphics at one point, but his unimaginative
lover assured him it was "just the mushrooms.")

They came to a windy plateau scattered with smooth black
rocks that had split into geometric shapes. At the edge of the
plateau, a six-foot stone obelisk rose—a man-made structure
which struck Michael as considerably less precise than the landscape it inhabited.

Douglas stood and stared at the stack of rocks. "It's very Carlos
Castaneda," he murmured.

"It's very phallic," said Gary.

"Well, don't just stand there." Ned grinned. "Worship it."

"Nah," said Gary, shaking his head. "It isn't big enough."

Their laughter must have traveled for miles. Ned began walking again, leading the way.

Michael caught up with him. "Was that it?"

"What?"

"The thing you wanted to show me?"

Ned shook his head with a cryptic smile.

They had yet another slope to climb, this one with a staggering view of the valley. Reddish stones arranged along the crest seemed to be fragments of a giant circle. "It used to be a peace symbol," Ned explained. "Remember those?"

As they scurried down the slope, Michael said: "That wasn't it, I guess?"

"Nope," answered Ned.

The terrain leveled out again, and they proceeded uncomfortably close to a crumbly precipice. The mushrooms were singing noisily in Michael's head, intensifying the experience. And distances were confusing in a land where the tiniest pebble resembled the mightiest mountain.

Suddenly, Ned sprinted ahead of the group, stopping near the edge of the drop-off. Michael was the first to catch up with him. "What the hell are you doing?"

"Look!" His partner laughed. He was crouching now, pointing to the valley floor beneath them where five brightly colored tents squatted like hotels on a Monopoly board. Behind them, shiny as a Dinky toy, was Ned's red pickup. They had circled back to the ridge above the campsite.

"Well?" asked Ned.

Michael peered down at the tiny tribal settlement and smiled. He didn't need to ask if this was Ned's surprise; he *knew* what Ned was saying: Look at us down there! Aren't we magnificent? Haven't we accomplished something? See what we mean to each other? It was a grand gesture on Michael's behalf, and he was deeply touched.

Ned cupped his hands and shouted hello to a Lilliputian figure standing by the campfire. It was Scotty, no doubt, already making preparations for lunch. He searched for the source of Ned's voice, then waved extravagantly. Ned and Michael both waved back.

After lunch, the group became fragmented again. Some with-drew for siestas and sex; others enjoyed the gentle downdrift of the mushrooms by wandering alone in the desert. Michael remained behind in the Big Tent, a solitary sultan engrossed in the silence. By nightfall, it seemed he had lived there forever.

He rose and walked toward the hills, following the pale ribbon of the creekbed through the mesquite trees. It was much cooler now, and fresh young stars had begun to appear in the deep purple sky. After a while, he sat down next to a cactus that was actually casting a shadow in the moonlight. A breeze caressed him.

Time passed.

He got up and headed back to camp, almost mesmerized by the amber luminescence of the Big Tent, the faint heartlike pulse of its walls, the gentle laughter from within. As he was about to enter, one of the canvas tarps trapped the rising wind like a spinnaker on a galleon, then ripped free from its restraints. Several people groaned in unison.

"Can I help?" he hollered.

"Michael?" It was Roger's voice.

"Yeah. Want me to make repairs?"

"Fabulous. It's over here. This back part just flapped open again."

"Where?" His hands fumbled in the shadows until he found the hole. "Here?"

"Bingo," said Gary.

Bringing the errant canvas under control, he laced the twine through the eyelets and pulled it tight. Then he made his way back to the front of the tent and lifted the flap.

They had dispensed with the Coleman lantern, having learned the night before that it didn't have a dimmer switch. Paul's inspired alternative was a heavy-duty flashlight in a brown paper bag, which was presently casting a golden Rembrandt glow on the six men sprawled across the Oriental rug Gary had received from his wife in their divorce settlement.

Gary sat against the ice chest, Roger's head resting in his lap. Douglas and Paul, the other pair of lovers, were idly rummaging through a pile of cassette tapes in the far corner of the tent. Ned was giving the hard-working Scotty a foot massage with Vaseline Intensive Care Lotion.

It was a charming tableau, sweet-spirited and oddly old-fashioned, like a turn-of-the-century photograph of a college football team, shoulder to shoulder, hand to thigh, lost in the first blush of male bonding.

"Thanks," said Gary, as Michael entered.

"No sweat," he answered.

Ned looked up from his labors on Scotty's feet. "You got some sun, bubba."

"Did I?" He pressed a finger to his biceps. "I think it's the lighting."

"No," Gary assured him. "It looks real good."

"Thanks." He entered and stretched out on the empty spot next to Ned and Scotty.

Scotty grinned at him blissfully. "There's some trail mix and cheese, if you're still hungry."

"No way," he replied.

After a brief exchange of eye signals, Roger and Gary rose, dusting off the seats of their pants. "Well, guys," said Roger, "it's been a long day . . . ."

"Uh-oh," piped Scotty. "We just lost the newlyweds."

Roger's embarrassment was heartrending. With a sudden stab of pain, Michael remembered the early days when he and Jon had been equally awkward about this maneuver. "Give 'em a break," said Ned, laughing. "They don't have a tent. They have to have privacy *sometime*."

"And they've been working like Trojans," added Douglas.

The departing Gary shot a look of amiable menace in Douglas's direction. "I'll get you for that."

"For what?" asked Scotty, after the lovers had left.

Douglas smiled. "Gary brought rubbers."

Three people said *"What?"* at the same time.

Douglas shrugged. "They don't call it a crisis for nothin'."

"Well, I know, but . . . " Scotty was almost sputtering. "Forget that. I'm willing to do my bit . . . but *c'mon.*"

Ned unleashed one of his mysterious grins. "I think they're kinda fun myself."

"Why?" asked Douglas. "Because they make you think of straight boys?"

"Marines," said Paul, embellishing on his lover's theme.

"I don't fantasize about straight men," Ned said flatly. "I've never sucked a cock that wasn't gay."

"So what's so great about them?" asked Scotty, his left foot still nestled in Ned's hands.

"Cocks?" asked Ned.

"Rubbers," grinned Scotty.

"Well . . . " Ned's nut-brown brow furrowed. "They're sorta like underwear."

"Calvin Klein Condoms," said Paul.

Everyone laughed.

"Why are they like underwear?" asked Scotty.

"Well . . . didn't you ever ask a guy to put his Jockey shorts back on just because it looked hot?"

"Yeah, sure, but . . . "

"And all there was between you and that incredible cock was this thin little piece of white cotton. So . . . that's kinda what rubbers are like. They get in the way, keep you from having everything at once. That can be the hottest thing of all."

Scotty rolled his eyes. "They are *balloons,* Ned. Face it. They will always be balloons. They are ridiculous things, and they are meant for *breeders.*"

23

More laughter.

"I remember," offered Douglas, "when the rubber machine always said 'For Prevention of Disease Only.'"

Paul looked at his lover. "They still do, dummy."

"But they always scratched out the 'Disease' part and wrote in 'Babies.' Now straight people don't even use them anymore."

"Yes they do."

"No they don't. They use the pill, or they get vasectomies or something."

While Douglas and Paul continued with this halfhearted quarrel, Michael signaled Ned, to indicate he was leaving. He slipped under the flap and made a beeline for his tent, avoiding even the slightest glance at the rise where Roger and Gary were encamped. He was almost there when a voice called out to him.

"Is that you, Michael?" It was Gary.

"Uh-huh."

"Come on over," said Roger.

He picked his way through the darkness until he found the path leading up to the rise. Only the moon lit the faces of the lovers, snuggled together under a zipped-open sleeping bag. "See"—grinned Roger—"we didn't run off to fuck."

"It must be the mushrooms," said Gary. "We've been telling ghost stories. It's really nice up here. Why don't you get your sleeping bag and join us?"

He looked back at the dark dome of his two-man tent, sitting empty under the stars. "I think I'll take you up on that," he said.

They fell asleep, the three of them, after Gary had told the one about the man with the hook . . .

CONDOMS, THEN AND NOW

William Matthews

Trojans, Sheik—the names confirmed what we feared:
sex happened elsewhere to blatant raptors.
Condoms? Those first years we called them rubbers.
Sometimes they broke, or slithered off, we heard,

if you "lost" your erection. (You don't
lose it, it melts.) (Alert readers have seen
how pronouns slither, too. What do I mean
by "you"?) We carried them in our wallets

as badges of fear. What fear had in store
for us, nobody guessed. The iron lung
years of UFOs and the Commie plague
were easy compared to a civil war —

now there's an oxymoron—between
the auto-immune system and the body
(sex then could be a sort of friendly
fire). "For protection from disease,"

the fine print said. For whom? From what?
We have met the enemy and they are us.

A BRIEF HISTORY OF CONDOMS

Kim Addonizio

1. *Origins of the American Condom*

The so-called American Condom (*Prophylacticus Americanus*) began behind the counters of druggists, springing to life in the dust and dark among prescription bottles.[1] In the diaspora which followed, some migrated into the air-conditioned light of Walgreens and Thriftys, others to the flickering fluorescent haze of convenience stores. Still others settled behind glass cabinets in large grocery chains. The most colorful varieties live crowded in baskets on the counters of medical clinics. Condoms thrive in great numbers throughout the continent of North America, and tend to be concentrated in large cities. Fundamentalist Christians and the occasional zealous Catholic have decreased their numbers slightly, but the overall impact of such predation has been insignificant on the population as a whole.

2. *Life Cycle of the Condom*

A condom is a simple one-celled organism which appears, at first

---

[1] The largely discredited "Big O Theory," first developed by Holstein, posits a divine origin, to wit: that the universe was originally the size and shape of a gigantic, cosmically conscious condom, which masturbated itself and exploded into particles which ripped it apart and sent particles streaming outward into space. There are still some elements of the scientific community who claim that there is an inner condom in each of us, remnant of the Great Rubber, and that we are reabsorbed into it at the end of earthly life. It's interesting to note that numerous mythologies of so-called primitive peoples offer variants of this proposition.

look, to be round and flat. When released from its foil "nest" and massaged, it changes its shape into a sock-like, membranous creature which clings to human flesh—specifically, the male's sexual organ. Condoms have a symbiotic relationship with humans; sperm released during human sexual activity is caught and eaten by the condom, allowing the condom to reproduce itself. Having fulfilled its evolutionary purpose, the condom then shrivels and dies. The fetus, or "conda," microscopic in size at this point, becomes airborne until it finds a suitable "nest," slips inside it and gestates in the warmth and protection the foil offers. A condom may lie dormant in its nest for years, but life outside the nest lasts from only a few minutes to half an hour or so.[2] It is fair to say that these brief moments, however, are by far the most gratifying; condoms have been observed to burst from sheer pleasure, and occasionally to squirm off of the male penis and travel excitedly upwards into the interior regions of the partner's body.[3]

3. *Common Uses of the Condom*

There are many valuable uses of the condom beyond the aforementioned use in sexual activity. Condoms may be filled with water and dropped from high windows to terrify old people; or loaded with jello and thrown at parties. They may be blown up like balloons. The flavored variety, once the lubricant is wiped away, is favored for eating by adolescent girls. Condoms may be

[2] The briefest known lifespan is .078 seconds; the longest, evidenced by a videotape of pornographic artist Jackoff Holmes, was well over an hour. Research has indicated that short-lived condoms tend to exhibit a high level of anxiety, whereas the longest-living emit alpha waves—an indication that, in human terms, these latter condoms tend to "stop and smell the roses," i.e. the odors of anal or vaginal secretions.

[3] Emergency Room records indicate that a small percentage of patients seek treatment, but the incidence is undoubtedly more frequent, according to anecdotal sources.

used in delaying sexual activity, as in, " I won't fuck you if I have to wear that thing on my dick."[4] Such a statement may have unfortunate results if the condom is then discarded, as it will simply dry up and die without reproducing itself. Condoms are dependent on human males, some of whom have an ambivalent relationship with them, and see them at best as a necessary evil.

4. *Inner Life of the Condom*
It is hard to ascertain whether a condom is capable of the emotions you and I regard as a part of sentient life. Does a condom experience depression, or fear death? Does it have a soul? If so, then we must examine carefully our treatment of this useful creature. Should it, for example, be so quickly relegated to the floor beside the bed, or the trash in the bathroom, or the weeds of the vacant lot? Perhaps our responsibility should extend to a decent burial, a few words said to mark the passing of our pleasure-seeking, short-lived friend. Perhaps it loves the woman whose vaginal walls drench it for a few minutes, or the man whose anus contracts around it. Perhaps it realizes that such bliss must soon, too soon, turn into pain and diminishment, into the awful isolation of the separate self. If the condom could speak, what truths might it tell us, privy as it is to some of our most intimate moments?

5. *One Condom's Story*
She carries me in her purse. She intends to be faithful, but just in case, she wants to be prepared. She is on a long trip, away from her lover. She meets a man who delights her, who is clever and interesting. He puts his hand on her hip as they are walking. They

---

[4] In the late twentieth century, this statement is an indication of gross stupidity on the part of the speaker. The best response to such an attitude is probably, "Go fuck yourself."

find a bar and drink until they can hardly stand up, then stagger to a hotel room. I hear them laughing and giggling, hear the rustle of clothes and good intentions being rapidly discarded. There is a blinding light as I am freed, feeling the cool air wash deliciously over me, and then I am lost in sensation, nothing matters but this, it is glorious, I am stretched taut, headed for that beautiful deadly opening; I go in and in. My head floods with sperm and I gorge myself, losing consciousness, and when I wake I find myself flushed down the pipes, along the sewers and out into the great river of the unborn, riding the currents down to the mothering sea.[5]

6. *Social Organization of Condom Communities*
There are many classes—one might even say castes—in the condom community. Brightly colored and flavored condoms are usually ostracized by those with a more uniform look and packaging. These second-class citizens are more likely to attempt to form what we can only call personal attachments with other condoms. Through a process known as "nest-ripping," two separate condoms may leak their lubricants and form a sort of gluey mass which causes the nests to bind to each other. They then become unfit for human use and hence unable to reproduce, so why this occurs remains an evolutionary mystery.[6]

7. *In Conclusion: A Personal Note*
There is much still to learn about this deceptively simple creature.

[5] The account is fictional; see Christopher Peckerwood's *I Am A Condom*. There is no authenticated stories of condoms speaking or writing their views, though apocryphal ones abound. Various people have claimed to be kidnapped by condoms from outer space, or to hear the voices of dead condoms speaking to them.
[6] For further readings see "Nest-ripping: Nature or Nurture?" in *Scientific American*; "Nest-Rippers, Menace to Society," ibid.; and the San Francisco journal *Honey, Let It Rip*.

I have here attempted the briefest outline of serious study and research. My own fascination began, perhaps, when as a boy I unrolled my first condom and jerked off into it, finding it a much neater method than rutting into the sheets my mother would have to wash. I have, frankly, never encountered a human body which gave me as much pleasure as the simple, unassuming condom, always eager to please, ready to take my jism and lap it up deliriously, then lie peacefully hanging from my penis while I relaxed with a cigarette. Several times during these jottings I have stopped to "denest" and massage one of the little creatures, to slip it over me and caress it, to squeeze and pull until we were both deliciously sated.[7] I confess to you now that I love them, that I think of nothing but their moist dripping bodies, that at night they come to me in my dreams, they hover over me and smile, and at last begin to speak.

---

[7] I can't get enough. Desire is endless. Sometimes I want to fuck everything in sight. I want to fuck the sheets, the trees outside my window, the men and women passing on the streets below; I want that ecstasy that only sex provides, the loss of self and finding of it, the *petit-morte* that tells me there is no true death, there is only connection and ceaseless change, there is only love against the darkness surrounding us, we are all ripped from the nest, helpless and exposed together; oh friends and colleagues, it all comes down to this: So many condoms. So little time.

EXCERPT FROM ROUSTABOUT: HOW I PAY

Michelle Chalfoun

WHILE THE REST of the circus sleeps, Jack Diamond, the fancy-trick roper, whips Marlboros from his wife Brandy's bruised and trembling lips.

They rehearse under the empty bigtop. While it's still early morning cool, before Tattoo Lou heats it up with horse practice, before Jay bosses his ringcrew to set the props and rake ringdirt.

Brandy is chained to the brightly scrolled bandstand. The wrist and ankle cuffs are plastic, painted to look like iron. Jack stalks around the ring, flashing malice and venom from his milky eyes. She's perfected a facial expression that reads of courage in the face of certain doom, even from the last row of the side grandstand. And he looks menacing and dangerous, twirling the rattlesnake whip over his thinning hair.

A sharp crack. A shower of sparks. Suddenly, miraculously, Brandy's lips are empty. Feigned openmouthed surprise from her, triumphant grin from him. He holds two halves of a neatly broken cigarette to his imagined audience. His hands will stop trembling by the matinee. He bows, he styles to his wife. She nods and smiles graciously at the empty bleachers. Her skin is pitted with tiny white pinholes. A thousand divots from fallen ash. Heavy pancake allows her to still get away with a low-cut gown. Her large chest, heaving with pretend fear, has always been one of the act's best assets. Some things never change.

Every morning, I wake to the crack of Jack's rattlesnake whip. I

could be sweating alone in the top bunk of my sleeper, or comfortable in the double-wide bed of Jayson's Country Squire. My
hips cradled inside his, my shoulders pressed against his warm
chest, his arm heavy and reassuring across my breast.

Crack. My eyes open.

Jayson's wall clock reads 6:25. Already too hot. The green dish
towel he uses as a curtain has slipped from the rod. Hot white sunlight littered with dust bakes my side of the bed. Half aroused, he
rolls my nipple between his thumb and finger. I stretch onto my
back. We shift in familiar ways. Then I'm beneath him. He kisses
my eyelids. Nose. Chin. My fingers play down the bumps of his
spine. Outside, the birds are already lulled to silence by the heat.
Though the air is still and breezeless, sounds drift in: Al fixing
breakfast in the cookhouse, banging pots, running water.
Someone cursing quietly from sleeper row. And the smells: salt
grease of old popcorn, garlic-rot of hotdogs decomposing under
the bleachers, vinyl coated canvas delaminating in the heat, elephant, horse, unwashed crew.

Jayson slides his tongue from one breast to the other. Like he's
licking an envelope, without thinking what's inside.

I wonder when my life will change.

For over three years now, since my fifteenth birthday, I've been
coming to Jayson's trailer. He knows my body so well his movements seem automatic. The same concentration as when he lubes
his Harley. He works from the top down. Lips, tits, clit, in. My
body still responds. I shouldn't complain. He kisses each of my
ribs. Brown curls brush my skin.

So if there are fifty-two weeks in a year, and we do it on aver-
age three or four times a week, that would be 3.5 times 52, then
that times 3 years; but then there's a half year more. I give up on
the math and roll my eyes to the pressboard trailer walls instead.

Before Jayson in the Country Squire, there was Pa in the

Airstream for six years. This began the night after Ma ran off. I was nine. He started slow at first, just a finger, then two. Then three. I don't remember exactly when Pa finally made me bleed. All I know is I didn't bleed just the first time. When I lay under Pa my head would bang against this one pressboard wall. If I tilted my head and rolled my eyes upward, I could watch the wall give a little with each thrust. A nailhead pushed its way out of the cheap pulp siding, and I watched it, imagined it working its way out a bit more each time my forehead banged against the wall. I made bets with myself: Who would fall out first, Pa or the nail? I remember trying mental telepathy. I'd chant in my head, "Out . . . Out . . . " The nailhead was still there when I packed my things and changed trailers.

Soon after my fifteenth birthday, Jayson noticed me hanging out wash behind Pa's silver-bullet Airstream. Perhaps he'd been sniffing around before; I remember his eyes sliding off my body when I looked up quickly in the cookhouse. Not like I'd have much chance to notice; Pa had threatened every crew member individually—if anyone touched his daughter, he'd cut off his balls and sew them shut in his mouth with seine twine.

Jayson is handsome in a way Pa wasn't. Jay is solid and confident: Pa was skinny and slippery. Pa never looked other men in the eye; Jay stares them down and bosses them around. Staying with Pa made me feel so dirty. Jayson is the ringcrew chief. I used to believe his protection would keep my name clean in all the gossips' mouths.

Later, Jayson told me he knew all along he could take Pa out, so he wasn't afraid. Defiant, he stood right outside Pa's Airstream and said "Hi." I said it back.

He walked around to me and lifted my sweaty hair off my neck. "You sure got beautiful hair," he said. I thought he was teasing: he could see it needed a wash. Then he lifted a torn pocket tee out the basket and pinned it to the line. We lifted a stained sheet together, his hand on one corner and mine on the other.

"You know, it doesn't have to be like this." He jutted his chin at a yellow stain.

"Bleach won't get them out. I tried."

He laughed. "I'm not talking about laundry." He kicked the bumper where Pa had put a sticker that said: "Don't come a-knockin' if the trailer's a-rockin'."

"That's none of your business." I snatched the wet sheet off the line and balled it up, threw it back in the basket.

He picked it out and hung it again. "You know I got my own trailer now."

"Congratulations. Hope you enjoy it."

"I'd enjoy it better with company." He clipped a clothespin on my tee-shirt, right above my heart.

I used it to hang a pair of Pa's briefs. "I don't know you well enough for that."

He laughed again. "Well, I'll move you in with Al. He'll play chaperon, till we get to know each other well enough."

I ran through the Airstream, stuffing my things into a garbage bag while Pa and Jayson squared off out front. I even took the bedspread, because I had sewed it. I was careful to leave nothing behind, except the pink plastic flamingos with their skinny steel legs stuck in the front lawn; I knew how much Pa hated them.

Eventually Pa and Jayson took to swinging at each other, and a crowd gathered, roustabouts and performers mingling in a way that only happens during fights. Jayson, clearly stronger, brought Pa to his knees. His ringcrew cheered him on. "She'll be rockin' Jay's trailer now!" I stepped out the trailer to the protection of Jayson's armpit. The peformer wives pretended to be weakened by the sight of Pa's bleeding lip. They covered their eyes with clean manicured hands. They spoke quiet French and Italian, as if chatting about the weather and the small audiences, as if they weren't standing in front of Pa's trailer, waiting, watching.

I walked through the crowd slow and graceful, like I was walking around the ring styling my costume. Tom, the canvas boss, held Pa at the elbows. Even so, Pa was shaking a sledgehammer handle and screaming at me, "You're gonna pay, you ungrateful bitch! You're gonna pay!"

Jay carried my bags to Al's sleeper. Al kissed me on both cheeks. "Sugar-booger, this is the girlfriend's sleeper now. We gonna have fun, just like sisters." To celebrate our sisterhood, he made cocktails out of champagne and raspberry liquor, and I swore never to live with another straight man again.

Now I was no longer supported by Pa, I had to work. I started in the costume truck with Tante. Sewing sequins back on leotards, patching fishnets worn down between the thighs by elephant hair. We disguised old costumes with feathers and tulle. We turned Tattoo Lou's horses into unicorns with satin-covered cardboard cones. Outside, the costume truck was bright white, painted with gold and red curlicues: *Fabrizio's Circus Fantastico*. Inside, it was damp wood walls with metal supports; bungee cords holding washers and dryers and racks of musty costumes. Buttons and rhinestones and ribbons, tangles of rich fabrics mildewing in the damp. I hated the dark cave, sitting all day. I'd grumble and Tante would scold. "Suffering is good for the soul. Jesus hung on the cross for three days until he died. Now he sits at the right hand of God. You should be so lucky." She'd stroke her yellow nails along the crinkled tissue of her burn-scarred skin. "You don't know what is suffering." She'd point to the eye patch covering her empty left socket. I knew she knew suffering. I knew she'd seen more with her one eye than most with two. She could tell me everything my ma never did.

Still, on moves, I wanted to be outside, on top of the tent

instead of folding sweat-stained costumes into bubble wrap. Before Jay's fight with Pa, Tom would take me up the laceline and sit me next to him on top of the mast, between the flags. He'd always spread his arms out like he owned the sky. "Best seat in the house," he'd say. Under the bigtop, we'd swing the quarterpole ropes round these heavy steel supports like fliers on trapeze. Setting up the tent was all energy and power. I wanted to be high in the air, legs wrapped around the mast, callus ripping on ropes and cables. I wanted to ride the bucking canvas, to wrestle it against the wind, lacing it tight, secure. I could tie all the knots, I could carry sidepoles on my shoulder, a hundred without dropping. I yelled "Hit it back!" loud as any man, and I could guy out the tent exactly, till it snapped into a perfect circle, tight as a drumskin. I tried to convince Tom to let me on the tent crew.

Tom said, "No openings."

"You could fit me in." I stomped around, hands on hips. "You taught me everything yourself. You know I'm good. It's 'cause I'm a girl."

He looked over my head. "It's 'cause you're Enis's girl. Wait till he calms down."

I didn't have to wait long. In his anger, Pa had been drinking round the clock, even during moves. He got meaner and sloppier, off balance all the time. Two weeks after I moved out, Pa fell off the top of the tent. I was sitting at the door of the costume truck, beading a cape, wishing I was up there, rigging. Pa's feet slipped out from under him. He hollered. I dropped my needle. Pa slid down the laceline, his yellow rainsuit slick on the plastic-coated canvas. When he hit the ground, his screams stopped short, like someone clicked off a radio mid-song. Tom, Jayson, and me leaned over his twisted body. A three foot round pool of blood circled his head, split wide open on a stake. Tom lifted Pa's wrist. Checked for a pulse. Pa's fingers fell back at unnatural angles. I figured he broke them grabbing at laces along the way, trying to stop his fall.

I pulled a Lucky from behind my ear and took Tom's lighter right out his pocket.

"You got an opening now," I said.

At Pa's funeral, the minister gave us a moment to remember Pa out loud. Damp wind blew through the thin cotton dress Al had lent me. We'd stuffed the toes of his black pumps with newspaper so they'd fit me, and now the heels sank into the muddy cemetery lawn. The minister cleared his throat.

Tom dropped his eyes to his boots. "Enis always worked hard."

Jay squeezed my hand. "We had our differences," he said.

Al touched his handkerchief to the corners of his dry eyes. "Excuse me." He blew his nose loudly.

Tante muttered in Arabic and made crosses over the grave.

I had nothing to say that should be said of the dead. I might've said, "Serves you right, bastard." I could've spit, "Ma and me were fine before you came along." I wanted to yell at the minister, "What the fuck you looking at?" But he didn't seem to want to be there any more than the rest of us. No performers had showed. Not even Tattoo Lou, though once she'd been tight with Ma, years ago. Ringmaster Fabrizio didn't even come. I just threw my handful of dirt on the casket. It thudded.

Jay and me stopped at a bar before going home. I had lots of Wild Turkeys. Jay bought them. The bartender never carded me. We drank and held hands across the booth. We followed overgrown train tracks back to the lot. I balance beam walked on the rail and he steadied me.

That night was our first time. After sex, my damp skin cooled except where we still touched. Jay smelled like bourbon, tobacco, and fresh dirt after rain. He kissed me everywhere for what seemed like hours. I felt like I knew why I was supposed to be alive. When I woke the next morning he was still holding me.

Back at the sleeper, Al shook his head. "Child, a man don't buy the cow when he gets the milk free."

I hung his dress back in the closet and changed into Carhartts. "I told Jay I won't move in with him till he marries me."

"You'll be waiting a long time, Girlfriend," Al said.

Over three years later, I'm still waiting.

Jayson finishes with my clit. I know what's next. I ask, "You got condoms?"

He stops moving over me and looks up.

"Shit, I forgot," he says.

He hovers there, thinking for a moment. Then he reaches over to the shelf and takes down some Corn Huskers lotion.

He knows I don't like it this way: it hurts more. But he's told me many times how it feels better. And he doesn't have to worry about getting me pregnant.

"Do you mind?" he asks. We know I won't refuse.

I shrug and roll over on my hands and knees. I think about relaxing. I concentrate on my breath. I look at the pressboard wall for exposed nailheads. When that doesn't work, I reach between my legs to hurry things along.

Later, in the Porta-John, I make a mental note to buy condoms. I picture attaching the note to my watch, just like Tom taught me. When I see my watch, I'll remember to go down the road to the drugstore.

In a perfect set-up, 152 stakes support the external structure of the bigtop: 120 spaced equally around the tent, one at each side-pole, plus four extra at each of the six lacelines, plus eight for the backstage extension. Each should hold equal tension, pulling the tent into a perfectly round circle. If any section weakens, even one stake, the bigtop's in danger.

No set-up is perfect. The ground's never completely level, and stakes pull from rain softened dirt. It's my job to watch the stakes for signs of weakness. I walk around the tent, inspecting for loose stakes that need backstaking, a second or third stake rigged to them for support. Tom thinks he taught me the proper way to drive stakes, but actually, Pa did. When I find a stake that's pulling, I measure the hole with my fingers. If two or more fingers fit in the hole with the stake, I drop one or more stakes, depending on what the hole needs, and a length of rope on the ground to mark it.

I walk back around the tent a second time, now with a 16-pound sledge, looking for those guylines where I preset more stakes and rope. I hold the new stake behind the old, at a slight angle so the head leans away from the tent, and tap it in place with short jerky taps, hand up near the head of the sledge. Then I stand up and back. Slide my hands to the end of the sledge handle, right hand above the left. Left leg forward, right leg back. Size up the swing with a slow practice arc. "This is important," Pa would say. "If you don't size up your swing, you may hit the stake with the wood and ruin a perfectly good handle."

I get my mark. The hammer swings down past my knees, up and around over my shoulders, and back down onto the stake. This full circle lets the sledge do the work. I can bury a stake with six strokes. Pa, who could do it in three, used to stand there counting my strokes. "Not bad for a girl," he'd say, "but not good enough."

Once, I heard him yelling at a new crew, "You a bunch of lazy-ass, First-of-May suckin'-on-your-mama's-teats New-Jacks! My little girl can drive stakes better one-handed." Some roustabout whose name I forgot or never even knew cracked, "What else can she do one-handed?" Pa laid him out with the sledgehammer handle. When he came to, Tom ran him off the lot. This still makes me smile whenever I think on it. I tie the first stake off to the backstake, smiling.

This work makes me proud. I like the way the sledge feels, I like the sound of the hammer on the stakes, and I like working alone. I feel strong, important. Sometimes I wish I could drive stakes all day, every day.

Back in the tent truck, I lean against the wall between the bent stakes and the fresh coils of yellow poly-pro. A cigarette. A chance to catch my breath. I rub my work warmed hands together, pleased with the thickness of my fingers, the hardness of my palms.

Between moves, it's my job to maintain the canvas. Open and close the tent for shows. Today I'm supposed to cut new lines for the horse tent. Looking for the heat gun, I run my eyes along the wall. Grommet kit, come-alongs, seine twine, and tieline. There's the hot-glue kit and Tom's ditty bag. My eyes fall on my watch. Condoms, I think. I'll do the lines later, during the show.

I check my pockets. A dollar and some change.

Back at the sleeper, I grab a fistful of pennies from Al's change drawer and my jacket off the bed. The wind has changed; it's cooled off some. Tom taught me to keep an eye on the weather; says weather knowledge is important for good tent management. Doesn't look like storm clouds. I slam the blue and red sleeper door shut, hop over the yellow security fence, and run towards town.

At the drugstore, I stare at the condom display. Naturlamb. Rough Rider. Ribbed for Her Pleasure. Hot Cinnamon. Wet 'n Wild. All hung on the wall behind the counter. I'll have to ask the old lady at the register to get me some. She is chicken skinny; her store apron collapses into her deflated chest. I can't read the price on any of them. I'm squinting at the prices when the lady says, "You decide?"

"Well, how much is the cheapest?" I meet her eyes.

"You can get a pack of three non-lubed Trojans for a buck fifty, but your boyfriend'll hate you when he's trying to put the damn thing on." I wonder how this dried up old prune could have such knowledge. And I wonder why she'd tell me. She probably gets off talking about condoms. Freak.

"Now, what I suggest is your reservoir tip with the nonoxynol-9 lubrication." She reaches for a black and gold box with two lovers walking into a sunset. "Pack of three for a dollar eighty-nine, the best you can get for that money." The box sits on the counter, and I read the gold script: For That Feeling of Love.

"Yeah, well, I'll take those. Whatever you just said." I start counting out change from my hand to the counter.

The chicken lady counts along with her eyes, and says, "All change?"

"No, there's a dollar." I lay the wrinkled bill on the counter along with the change. Jesus. Like it matters how I pay.

"Well, a girl's gotta pay for her fun somehow." She drops the box into a small brown bag and rings up my purchase. "Gotta protect herself." She titters into her hand, then touches her hair lightly, patting it like she just found a poodle resting on her head. I can't get out of there fast enough. The spongy mat in front of the door sings "Bing-bong," announcing my exit. The "bong" cuts off sharply.

Outside, the bright sun sparkles off the green and brown glass embedded in the street. Like Tante has come through and hot-glued rhinestones to the asphalt. The clouds have blown off, but the breeze has picked up. I'm glad to have my jacket. The air smells suburban. Cut grass, pool chlorine, backyard cookout char-coal. I consider wandering around town a bit, maybe buying myself a soda and a magazine. Then I realize I don't have any more money. Still, I could sit on a green wooden bench and watch people. I could window shop. Or even wander through the stores, touching things. Take clothes off the rack and hold them against my body, hanger and all. When the store ladies ask me if I need help, or even look at me funny, I could say, "I'm just browsing," like Ma used to when we went out shopping together. If I found a beautiful dress, I'd buy it, and wear it home so Jayson would see how pretty I look. He'd tell me I was beautiful, and he'd maybe ask me out. We could go to dinner, or go dancing. At the end of the evening, he'd drop me off at my sleeper door and we'd kiss good night. Like a real date.

A dummy in the window of Young Miss Fashions wears a flow-ered dress with fabric so light it's nearly see-through. It would float when I walked. The square of cardboard hanging from the sleeve says $78. A woman looks through the dusty window at me. Her fingers rest lightly on the window dress. Our eyes meet. One thick nickel warms in my palm. I decide I don't really want to be inside, shopping. It's too beautiful out. Warm in the sun and cool in the shade. I consider walking up and down the side streets, looking at the houses and the yards, wondering about the families inside.

Instead I keep on walking along the main street, past the school and onto the main road. Where the houses and stores end, the road begins to look like an interstate, except for the flowers on the median strip. I walk with traffic, even though the circus lot is on the other side of the street. It's down a ways, about a half mile, and there's no sidewalk on that side of the road. Just a thin strip of grass and a tall twist wire fence. The steel wire forms diamond-shaped holes.

I walk slowly, enjoying the air, eyes fixed on the white and blue tent in the distance. Bright flags wave in the breeze. I'd go to that show if I lived in town. I think of kids coming home from school clutching free tickets the 24-hour man passed out at recess, that scrap of red cardboard nearly melting in their hot wet hands. Begging their folks over suppers of pork chops and collard greens, "Can we go please?" The folks give in and buy five more tickets for the rest of the family, just because the advance man gave little Suzie a free one while she hung from the monkey bars.

I wonder what Al's making for lunch and whether Tom has any projects for this afternoon. Straightening stakes maybe? Probably those horse tent lines. If not, maybe I could come back into town and do me and Jayson's laundry. He'd give me quarters. Maybe Al would come too.

A red van slows down beside me. "Hey, circus lady."

I almost flinch, but I recover before my body gives me away. I keep walking. Except for a small sideways flick out the corner of my eye, I ignore the two guys waving at me.

"Hey, are you the lion tamer? You want to tame my lion, lady?" The guy on the passenger side is leaning out the window and banging his hand against the door of the van.

"You know how to charm a cobra?" I wonder how they know I'm from the show. Then I realize I'm wearing my tour jacket. My face goes hot, armpits sticky. I'd take off my jacket, but I don't want to carry it. Pa taught me in such a situation I should always keep my hands free.

"Maybe she's a freak." "Yeah, are you a freak? You got three tits or something?" They're both talking and laughing now, inching along at my pace.

Cars honk and pass them; they're stopping traffic. They look about 20, 21; one guy has dark hair. The van inches along so close I'm sure the dark haired guy could touch my left shoulder if he leaned out the window a bit. I move onto the grass. It would be stupid to run, I think. Goddamn townies.

"Freak me, baby." My heart stalls, restarts a moment later with a loud thump. Sweaty palms stain the paper bag.

"Freak me, baby." "Freak me, fuck." "Fuck me, freak." My skin tightens. They're so loud. Stop. Please stop, I want to scream.

"Fuck me, you fuckin' freak!"

I duck behind the van. Run across the street. A pickup shoots past my hips, the driver cursing me. I feel better now that they are on the other side of the road. Still, I find myself trying to walk quickly, but the grass strip behind the fence is narrow; my feet stumble a little, kicking up divots. I stare into oncoming traffic. The cars and trucks drive towards, then past me, a foot from my shoulder.

Across the road, the red van picks up speed again, moves with traffic. I watch it drive away. Up ahead there's a break in the median strip. The red van pulls a U-turn through the break and heads back towards me. I think: They can't do anything but drive by; I'm facing oncoming traffic, what can they do?

The red van pulls up alongside me and stops. A blue sedan honks and swerves around them, its driver yelling something I don't hear.

"Hey, mama, don't be so cold. you aren't being very nice now, are you?" The passenger talks at me while the driver concentrates on driving backwards and slow. They'll get tired of this fast, I think. Just don't look, I think. My focus sharpens. Unnecessary images disappear. I concentrate on the tent getting larger, too slowly. My vision narrows to only the tent and the van.

"She's not being very nice, is she Jack? My mama says circus people aren't nice, says they live like animals. You like an animal?" He growls at me, then barks. The hairs on my neck and forearms raise off my skin. Like a dog's.

Another car drives around them, laying on the horn. Where are all the highway cops?

"I wanna teach you how to be nice, circus lady." The dark-haired passenger opens the door. The edge hits my shoulder. My mind goes blank. My body becomes a machine.

Fence. Muscles snap. I throw my bag over the top and stick my toes and fingers through the diamond-shaped holes. Kick the hand reaching for my ankle and grab for the silver twist-tops of the fence. Don't listen to the dark haired one yelling. Swinging my left leg over, I feel my jeans catch, then rip.

When I bend down to pick up my bag, I hear, "That bitch is crazy. Let's get outta here."

The drugstore bag is very red. I look at my right hand, it's very red too. The pinkie has fallen away from the bone. Yellow globs of fat fall past the red and white gristle to the grass. There is yellow fat in my hand. Where is the pain? So much blood . . .

Blood.

Time slows. A lightness fills my head. The silver fence glitters and shines. Tears on my eyelashes draw a rainbow halo around the distant tent. I don't feel like I'm crying, yet there are tears dropping. But I feel just fine, like I'm floating. When I get to the tent, everything will be okay.

I tuck the bag in my pocket with my clumsy left hand then wrap this left hand around the bloody right one. It registers that the flesh is all there, just sliced neatly, peeled back like a banana skin. I put pressure on my hand and hold both over my head. My feet skim the ground. I'm flying towards the lot. I don't look back to see if the townies are still there.

"Just breathe, keep breathing." Jayson looks over at me so often I worry he'll drive off the road. I lean my head against the cool glass of the Suburban. My hand's raised above my heart, propped up on the dashboard.

He says, "Shit. Mat, how're you gonna work now? That was

stupid, real stupid." I don't know what kind of answer he wants.

"What exactly happened?"

"Some guys were bugging me on the road, so I went over the fence." I close my eyes.

"Hey now, hey. Don't go to sleep. Keep breathing. Tell me what happened." He looks over at me again. Maybe he is worried.

"They were following me in their van."

"So why didn't you cross the road?"

"I did, but they did too. They drove backwards, against traffic, to keep yelling at me." I really can't explain this, I think. Already it makes no sense to me.

"Did they touch you? Did the fuckers touch you? I swear . . . " He tries to think of something he can do. Make them pay. For a moment my eyes tear up. I blink and then stare at the continuous white line of guardrail streaming past my window.

"No, I got over the fence. My hand just got caught on those twisty wires on top is all." I feel kind of cold.

"You okay?" Jayson looks at me again. It takes me a while to answer, so he asks again.

"I'm fine. A little cold is all." I want to lie down. Instead I say, "I'm glad Tom gave us the production vehicle. I don't think I could've stayed on your motorcycle. Tom's so nice..."

"Yes, he's nice."

"You're nice too." My voice is sleepy.

"Yes, I'm nice too." He looks over at me, and I smile back slowly.

"I'm nice too, Jayson." I feel very nice.

"You're nice too, Matty." He looks at me. His forehead is wrinkled in a way that makes him look old and sad.

"Don't look so worried. I can't feel my hand now. It doesn't hurt anymore."

"That's good, that's good. You're gonna be fine, fine."

"Fine."

"Don't go to sleep now."

"No, I'm fine," I say. I feel fine. Numb.

"How are you going to pay?" The secretary nurse shuffles papers. She's all in white. She has many forms for us to fill out before they'll take me in.

"Don't know." I don't know if I said that out loud or not. I feel cold again. Sleepy. Stay awake, look around. On the wall a poster shows a naked woman in profile. Her body is see-through, her internal organs covered with layers of fat. Fat coats her body. The artist colored the fat yellow, and it looks just like what fell out my finger. The heading reads: "Fat, the Leading Cause of Today's Health Problems."

"Workman's comp. She got workman's comp from the circus. Where's your wallet, honey?" Jayson starts feeling in my jacket pockets.

"In my back pocket, silly." I giggle. I feel his hand in my pocket, and that makes me giggle more.

"Name?" the nurse asks. Pen taps the clipboard. She doesn't seem to like her job much.

"That's Jayson," I tell her.

She looks disgusted. Or bored. "No, ma'am. I mean you, the patient."

"Oh, sorry." I want to know when we're going to leave. I don't feel so great. I want to go to sleep. "I want to go to sleep." I tell Jayson, but he isn't listening, he's talking to the nurse.

"Listen, lady, can we do something here? My girlfriend's in shock or something. She could lose that finger. Just get her a doctor and I'll fill out any goddamn form you want."

"You called me your girlfriend. He called me his girlfriend." I tell the nurse.

Jay brushes his knuckles across my forehead. Tucks my hair

behind my ears. "You're my girl, aren't you?" He's staring at the wall behind the nurse. He answers himself. "You're my girl."

The nurse secretary flips around the clipboard and points to a line with an X. "Okay, just as long as she signs here."

I try to pick up the pen, but my right hand isn't working. My left hand's stuck to it. I try again, but I can't seem to separate my hands. Instead I start to cry. "I can't sign it, Jayson, I can't. What's wrong with my hand?"

"Here now. Nothing's wrong." He lays his hand on top of my two stuck together hands and helps me make an X.

"There, you happy now?" The clipboard scuttles across her desk, scattering pens, papers. I don't see why Jayson is being so mean to the nurse.

"Why are you being so mean?" I call back over my shoulder. A large man in white leads me down the hall.

The male nurse sits me down. His hands are heavy on my shoulders. "Where's Jayson? I need Jayson here."

He doesn't answer. He plunges my hand in a basin of yellow disinfectant. My hands come apart, and I scream.

Later, cops show up on the lot. One older, heavier; one young, blond, and slim. I meet them in the cookhouse with Jayson. Al offers us all coffee. He takes extra time pouring the younger cop's cup. He sings, "I love a man in uniform," lightly under his breath. I stare at the white gauze bandage on my hand, waiting for something to begin. My pinkie has 21 stitches; I wonder if I can take them out myself, or if I'll have to go back to a hospital.

"Well, ma'am, do you want to press charges?" This comes from the young blond cop. He has a notebook and pen. The older cop concentrates on rolling a Drum cigarette. The young cop doesn't look much older than 18. He can't be much older than me.

"Yeah, we want those bastards to pay. Look at what they did to

50

Mat here." Jayson points at my hand. It looks impressive with so much bandage.

"She works with her hands, you know; she's a rigger," Al calls from his corner.

"Who's this?" asks the older cop. He licks the paper to seal his cigarette.

"My sleeper mate," I say. Al winks at the young blond. The older cop grunts and spits a thread of tobacco.

"Well, Nelly"—he glances towards Al and smiles at his young partner—"that's something for lawyers, later, if you sue. We only deal with relevant facts."

"Any witnesses?" The young cop's pen hovers over his clip-board.

I think of the cars that drove by without stopping. "No," I answer.

"Just exactly what happened?" He lifts his pen again.

"Well, they were following me in their van and yelling things at me, so I crossed the street to get away. They pulled a U-turn and started driving backwards against the traffic in order to continue bothering me."

"What do you mean by bothering, exactly?" The young cop hasn't written anything yet.

"You know, like 'Hey, baby' and whatnot." I don't feel like getting into it for these guys.

"Did they touch you?" The old cop asks this.

"Well, the passenger got out the van . . ."

"Yes, but were you ever touched?" The young one only writes now, the older one asking all the questions.

"Only by the van door."

"So no one ever touched you?"

"No, I got away before they got a chance to."

"So how did you get injured?"

"Climbing over the fence. You know, to get away." I shake a cig-arette out of my pack with my left hand, but I don't put it to my lips. Instead I roll it around the table with my bandaged hand.

The cookhouse walls are transparent vinyl. Outside, the con-cessionaires open up their tents. They concentrate on attaching balloons to strings, fuzzy toy monkeys to sticks. No one looks towards us.

"So those boys did not cut you: you cut yourself by accident, climbing a fence." The old cop finally lights his Drum.

I concentrate on pushing my cigarette around on the table. Eventually I look up and say, "I got cut because I had to climb over the fence fast, to get away. So they wouldn't do anything to me." A few bars of "Rock the Casbah" blast through the air. Sound check. Soon the lot will open to the public.

"Well . . . " The cop sucks his Drum and blows smoke rings, clicking his jaw once for each ring. "How do we ever know what someone is gonna do, right? I mean, I would think when you take a cigarette out of a pack you're gonna smoke it, but look, here you are just pushing it around the table." He gestures at me with his Drum between his short thumb and forefinger. "Get my point?" he says.

I look at Jayson. I can't believe he isn't saying anything. I pick up the Lucky Strike and clench it between my teeth. Tobacco squeezes out onto my tongue. I talk around it while I search my pockets with my clumsy left hand.

"They threatened me. I know they wanted to do something to me. Isn't that something?" I look at Al, and he sashays over slow to light my cigarette with a coy flick of his lighter. I release a big drag at the old cop.

"Well," says the old cop, "as I see it, some town boys see an attractive circus lady"—his eyes slide across my breasts—"and they want to get to know her. You know you shouldn't walk unaccompanied in a strange town, don't you? And with these two men to protect you . . . " He looks at Al, and the young cop smiles. "What were you doing out by yourself on a Friday morning in a strange town, hmmm?"

Buying condoms, I say to myself.

"Besides, there is no way I can arrest some boys for intent to do something, now can I?"

I sit with my mouth open. When I finally think to shut it, I can hear my teeth come together hard. I wonder if they could hear that outside my mouth. "So you're saying the only way I could press charges would be if they touched me?"

"Well, actually, only if you could prove they touched you in a malicious way. And unfortunately, there were no witnesses." He smiles at the younger cop, no longer pretending to take notes.

"Maybe I should've stood there and let them hurt me so I'd have a case. But I guess that wouldn't be good enough. I mean, no one stopped to witness." I want to yell this, but I only speak softly.

"Now, ma'am, there's no need to get angry. I realize you're a little hysterical after your scare. But that's all it was. A little scare." He leans forward in his chair and holds his finger and thumb like he's pinching the air. His uniform pants stretch tight across his lap. A small bulge, too far down on his left thigh to make sense, gags me. He follows my eyes. I want to throw hot coffee and watch him shrivel. His hand pats my forearm once. I shake him off.

"What I'm saying is, there's little chance a lady"—he smiles at the young cop—"a lady like yourself would have much of a case against some local boys who were just being friendly."

Jayson straightens up the Country Squire, picking up clothes and smelling them. Some he throws in a green nylon stuff sack, some he folds and puts back in the drawer. I'm sitting on the foldout bed. Cradling my hurt hand with my good hand. He explains to me that people can get arrested for assault with intent to kill. This I already know, because Tante's husband was arrested for that after he burned her, or so she says. But there is no law against harassment with intent to rape, he continues. At least not here. Not with street encounters . . .

I listen to the rhythm of his words playing against the clown walkabout music. A light roar from the tent. Jacomo has just thrown confetti on the front row; they thought it would be water.

. . . maybe in offices . . . but not on streets . . . free speech . . . take it as a compliment . . .

Jayson moves around the trailer, looking for anything he might have missed. "What were you doing anyhow, Mat? In town, on a show day?"

I think of what Ma used to say: "If he's trying to buy, you must be advertising."

"Hey, Jay," I say under my breath but loud enough for him to hear, "you forgot to say I was asking for it."

He straightens up and drops a shirt from his hands. "Jesus, Mat, whose fault was it? Mine?"

His back twitches. The audience roars.

"You didn't have condoms. I was buying condoms, so maybe you'd face me for once." I wait. Something will happen now.

He turns with his fist raised. Dust sparkles past my eyes on a stream of sunlight. His fist breaks through the shiny particles and sends them dancing away.

Inches from my face, he turns. Hits the wall clock. It shatters. I don't move. The air vibrates around me.

For a long while he stares at the blood on his knuckles.

"I face you." His knuckles are bleeding. His bottom lip is pushed out. "I always face you. The whole time except for that one thing."

I feel so tired. I don't have energy to argue. Nothing changes.

"Sorry," I say.

"No, I'm sorry."

"It's okay. It's fine," I say.

"It's just this all just makes me so mad." He waves his bloody hand weakly, gesturing at nothing in particular, maybe at everything in general. "And I hate it when you put words in my mouth," he says quietly.

"Sorry."

"Don't say that if you don't mean it."

"No, Jay, I'm really sorry."

"Then why did you say that?"

"Sorry, Jayson, I guess it's just been a hard day."

"Yeah, well, I had to miss ringset to drive you. I was worried. I was worried and I missed ringset. How do you think that made me feel?"

"Sorry, Jayson. Sorry."

I hold myself very still while he washes the blood off his knuckles. He should be in the tent, wearing his tux, directing the ringcrew. But he's here with me. And I really need him here. I really need him to be nice. I need to be held, rocked, touched gently. Anything. Anything to get me out of my head, which keeps replaying the day.

He hands me a Band-Aid and I stretch it across his cut. My bandaged hand feels stiff and fat, and I don't do a good job.

The juggling music begins. His lips move as he counts the acts left in the show. I don't want to be alone.

I say, "Jay, I really want to thank you for taking me to the hospital."

He puts his hand on my knee. "Anytime."

"No, really, thank you," I say again, holding his tee-shirt at the neck with my left hand.

He smiles down at me. I notice his cheeks and lips sag when he leans over, making him look older than his thirty-five years.

"Can I repay you?" I ask, teasing. His eyes rest on the tux hanging on the closet door. Clumsy with bandage, I unbuckle his belt. His eyes slide away from the tux.

"Sure. I'll take it out in trade," he says, helping me with his belt.

The show's over. Tom laces the back door flap shut. Under the horse tent, Tattoo Lou brushes her animals. Her assistant polishes the silver. He hangs the clean tack off the lines I never replaced. A wasted afternoon. When I pass the stakeline, I check for pulled stakes. All the guylines are secure, but I wish they weren't, so I could drive more stakes. Then I realize I couldn't swing a sledge with my gimpy hand. I kick the steel stairs on my way in the sleeper. They clang once in protest. Halfway in, I decide I need to walk. I slam the door shut. I don't care where I go, just away from the lot, away from town.

The wind lifts my hair off my neck, and I think about shaving it off. My muscles tighten and relax with each step, and I imagine getting fat; protective yellow globs coating my internal organs, shielding me. Sun on my skin, I think about burning it off and leaving shiny tight scars, like Tante's. I jump over the security fence and pick up the pace. Imagine growing in my armpit hair, my leg hair, and getting so strong my body looks more like a man's than a woman's. Cutting off my breasts, sewing myself shut. I think about my child's body under Pa's and wonder what I advertised then, with my hairless flat self.

Running now, running. I think about Pa, the nailhead, falling, falling out. How I called Pa's penis "him" as if it had its own brain. How else could Pa be so different, with two different halves of himself? Out of breath, I slow to a walk. My pinkie throbs with my slowing heart.

I turn around and walk back to the show. I concentrate on my breath, my heart. I collapse inwards. Focus on milkweed seeds blowing past my eyes. A meaningless pattern of white. Something to get lost in.

At home, I stand on Al's bunk to reach the top of the wall unit, where he stores his precious Cabernet Sauvignon. He calls it "Cab Salve." There are three bottles. Enough for me. Tomorrow I'll go back to town to replace them.

FLUSH

William Feustle

I AM SITTING on the edge of the tub naked, holding it in my hand. Each night I wait until I hear that particular little catch of breath, a small soft noise that she makes before her breathing goes slow and regular. What is that noise? I worry about it.

I slid out of bed and took it off. Easy on, easy off. She used to reach over and pull it off of me, jump out of bed, and come back to snuggle against my warmth. She stopped. I worry about it. I picture her turning it inside out, massaging and pushing its trapped liquids into her waiting womb, the ticking of the biological clock deafening her caution. I would look in the trash can in the mornings but they were never there. Maybe she flushed them. Or maybe she saved them up in the freezer wrapped in aluminum foil and deceptively labeled hot dogs or chicken or pork chops. Saved up until she had enough for what? And why has she stopped?

I lift the lid of the toilet and start to drop it in. I can picture it twirling around and around as it starts its whitefish migration down the pipes. I worry about it. I can picture it caught on some rusty bump on the inside of my old pipes, open, filling with water, swelling like a balloon angioplasty, thoroughly blocking the flow. Too strong to break. Water backing up all over the bathroom. Or, if it moved farther down the line, sewage backing up in both bathrooms, or the whole neighborhood. Trucks and men with spotlights and long metal snakes searching out the blockage, pulling it out, holding it up to the cheering crowds like a trophy large-mouth bass.

I knot the end and pull it tight. I picture the sewage treatment plant. I can see the worker using a net to fish them all out. I worry about it. He's wearing, no, she's wearing a brown uniform. What other color could it be. She's heavy-set, stocky, and her dark hair pulled severely back and tied recklessly in a pony tail. As she scoops, she remembers leaving her young fair-haired lover abandoned among tousled sheets, her firm small-nippled breasts barely covered by the thin cotton. Never have a child of our own she thinks as she scoops them, once filled with life and now with waste, into a white plastic bucket. Both of them turned down period after period for artificial insemination. Shit happens, she thinks. Then one carefully knotted, its contents uncontaminated. She digs it out, dirtying her hand which she wipes on her brown uniform. She puts it in her pocket, washes it off in the ladies room, packs it in her brown paper lunch bag in the small refrigerator. A chance she thinks, no paperwork, no questions. Maybe contaminated, maybe deadly. She takes it home and lovingly ejects its contents into her lover.

Miracles happen. A child forms. My child. I don't even know that it, he, my bastard son, exists. He wonders why his mommy and daddy are both mommies. His friends pick on him. I worry about it. He learns enough to wonder about who his father really is. A man sitting naked, pondering a knotted condom never enters his mind. Movie stars, Axl Rose, American Gladiators are what he pictures. He grows and becomes famous. I watch him one night being interviewed by Jay Leno totally unaware that he is my son, and then climbing out of bed, I die cold and alone in a bathroom.

I stand up and slip on the rug. It scoots out from under my feet on the tile floor, its rubber backing worn from age. I sit back down hard on the side of the tub. I feel the impact as a sharp pain along my spine. I worry about it. It goes away and I try standing again, make it this time and open the medicine cabinet. With the little cuticle scissors, I cut the knotted end off and watch it drop into the toilet bowl. I start to drop the remainder in after it but remember the clogged sewer line. I once saw a show on safe sex where the narrator stretched a condom first over one hand, then over the other, then pulled his condom-clad hands over his head, down over his nose, the latex stretching almost clear. With the condom over both hands and head, he exhaled through his nose, inflating the condom until it shot off his head and buzzed across the room. Strong little bastards. I cut the tip off with the small scissors and drop the pieces into the commode.

I think about getting a new condom and pulling it over my head, working it up as a party trick or something, but I picture myself being unable to blow it off, slowly suffocating. I worry about it. The ambulance crew, when it finally arrives, finds me dead and blue and naked, my hands tightly clasped over my ears, held in place by the still intact condom, my eyes rolled back into my head. They load me on a stretcher and carry me down the steps. In front of the house, a crowd of neighbors, drawn to the flashing lights like moths, hovers to watch the excitement. The sheet covering my body catches on the worn copper weather stripping of my front door and is yanked off. The two attendants try to untangle it and I lie on the stretcher on my front porch naked and blue while my neighbors titter at my latex bound head and hands.

I start to flush the toilet, and remember how much water I'm wasting. Five gallons a flush? More? I worry about it. It can wait until tomorrow morning's additions. What was that they said in New York a few years ago, if it's yellow let it mellow, if it's brown, flush it down. What if it's latex? I stare at the three pieces. They float on the surface, making small undulations like a jellyfish mom and her two smaller offspring. If I don't flush will she wonder why it's in three pieces? If I do flush will it wake her up? I flush. The toilet seems extremely loud, a ferocious rush, a gigantic gurgle, the incessant running of water to fill the tank.

I turn out the bathroom light and am blinded. I feel my way back to the bed and climb in. She rolls over and pulls the sheet up over my shoulders. Did I wake you? I ask. Don't worry about it, she tells me. She reaches her hand down between my legs. I feel in the open night table drawer for the familiar package.

John Irving

"How do you know you're going to be a writer," Cushie Percy asked him once.

It was Garp's senior year and they were walking out of town along the Steering River to a place Cushie said she knew. She was home for the weekend from Dibbs. The Dibbs School was the fifth prep school for girls that Cushie Percy had attended; she'd started out at Talbot, in Helen's class, but Cushie had disciplinary problems and she'd been asked to leave. The disciplinary problems had repeated themselves at three other schools. Among the boys at Steering, the Dibbs School was famous—and popular—for its girls with disciplinary problems.

It was high tide on the Steering River and Garp watched an eight-oared shell glide out on the water; a sea gull followed it. Cushie Percy took Garp's hand. Cushie had many complicated ways of testing a boy's affection for her. Many of the Steering boys were willing to handle Cushie when they were alone with her, but most of them did not like to be *seen* demonstrating any affection for her. Garp, Cushie noticed, didn't care. He held her hand firmly; of course, they had grown up together, but she did not think they were very good or close friends. At least, Cushie thought, if Garp wanted what the others wanted, he was not embarrassed to be seen pursuing it. Cushie liked him for this.

"I thought you were going to be a wrestler," Cushie said to Garp.

"I *am* a wrestler," Garp said. "I'm *going* to be a writer."

"And you're going to marry Helen Holm," Cushie teased him.

"Maybe," Garp said; his hand went a little limp in hers. Cushie knew this was another humorless topic with him—Helen Holm—and she should be careful.

A group of Steering boys came up the river path toward them; they passed, and one of them called back, "What are you getting into, Garp?"

Cushie squeezed his hand. "Don't let them bother you," she said.

"They don't bother me," Garp said.

"What are you going to write about?" Cushie asked him.

"I don't know," Garp said.

He didn't even know if he was going to college. Some schools in the Midwest had been interested in his wrestling, and Ernie Holm had written some letters. Two places had asked to see him and Garp had visited them. In their wrestling rooms, he had not felt so much out classed as he had felt out*wanted*. The college wrestlers seemed to want to beat him more than he wanted to beat them. But one school had made him a cautious offer—a little money, and no promises beyond the first year. Fair enough, considering he was from New England. But Ernie had told him this already. "It's a different sport out there, kid. I mean, you've got the ability—and if I do say so myself, you've had the coaching. What you haven't had is the competition. And you've got to be hungry for it, Garp. You've got to really be interested, you know."

And when he asked Tinch about where he should go to school, for his *writing*, Tinch had appeared at a typical loss. "Some g-g-good school, I guess," he said. "But if you're going to w-w-write," Tinch said, "won't you d-d-do it anywhere?"

"You have a nice body," Cushie Percy whispered to Garp, and he squeezed her hand back.

"So do *you*," he told her, honestly. She had, in fact, an absurd body. Small but wholly bloomed, a compact blossom. Her name, Garp thought, should not have been Cushman but *Cushion*—and since their childhood together, he had sometimes called her that. "Hey, Cushion, want to take a walk?" She said she knew a place.

"Where are you taking me?" Garp asked her.

"Ha!" she said. "*You're* taking *me*. I'm just showing you the way. And the place," she said.

They went off the path by the part of the Steering River that long ago was called The Gut. A ship had been mired there once, but there was no visible evidence. Only the shore betrayed a history. It was at this narrow bend that Everett Steering had imagined obliterating the British—and here were Everett's cannons, three huge iron tubes, rusting into the concrete mountings. Once they had swiveled, of course, but the later-day town fathers had fixed them forever in place. Beside them was a permanent cluster of cannon balls, grown together in cement. The balls were greenish and red with rust, as if they belonged to a vessel long undersea, and the concrete platform where the cannons were mounted was now littered with youthful trash—beer cans and broken glass. The grassy slope leading down to the still and almost empty river was trampled, as if nibbled by sheep—but Garp knew it was merely pounded by countless Steering schoolboys and their dates. Cushie's choice of a place to go was not very original, though it was like her, Garp thought.

Garp liked Cushie, and William Percy had always treated Garp well. Garp had been too young to know Stewie Two, and Dopey was Dopey. Young Pooh was a strange, scary child, Garp thought, but Cushie's touching brainlessness was straight from her mother, Midge Steering Percy. Garp felt dishonest with Cushie for not mentioning what he took to be the utter assholery of her father, Fat Stew.

"Haven't you ever been here before?" Cushie asked Garp.

"Maybe with my mother," Garp said, "but it's been a while." Of course he knew what "the cannons" were. The pet phrase at Steering was "getting banged at the cannons"—as in "I got banged at the cannons last weekend," or "You should have seen old Fenley blasting away at the cannons." Even the cannons themselves bore these informal inscriptions: "Paul banged Betty, '58" and "M. Overton, '59, shot his wad here."

Across the languid river Garp watched the golfers from the Steering Country Club. Even far away, their ridiculous clothing looked unnatural against the green fairway and beyond the marsh grass that grew down to the mudflats. Their madras prints and plaids among the green-brown, gray-brown shoreline made them look like cautious and out-of-place land animals following their hopping white dots across a lake. "Jesus, golf is silly," Garp said. His thesis of games with balls and clubs, again; Cushie had heard it before and wasn't interested. She settled down in a soft place— the river below them, bushes around them, and over their shoulders the yawning mouths of the great cannons. Garp looked up into the mouth of the nearest cannon and was startled to see the head of a smashed doll, one glassy eye on him.

Cushie unbuttoned his shirt and lightly bit his nipples.

"I like you," she said.

"I like *you*, Cushion," he said.

"Does it spoil it?" Cushie asked him. "Us being old friends?"

"Oh no," he said. He hoped they would hurry ahead to "it" because *it* had never happened to Garp before, and he was counting on Cushie for her experience. They kissed wetly in the well-pounded grass; Cushie was an open-mouthed kisser, artfully jamming her hard little teeth into his.

Honest, even at this age, Garp tried to mumble to her that he thought her father was an idiot.

"Of course he is," Cushie agreed. "Your mother's a little strange, too, don't you think?"

Well, yes, Garp supposed she was. "But I like her anyway," he said, most faithful of sons. Even then.

"Oh, *I* like her, too," Cushie said. Thus having said what was necessary, Cushie undressed. Garp undressed, but she asked him, suddenly, "Come on, where is it?"

Garp panicked. Where was *what*? He'd thought she was holding it.

"Where's your *thing?*" Cushie demanded, tugging what Garp thought *was* his thing.

"What?" Garp said.

"Oh wow, didn't you bring any?" Cushie asked him. Garp wondered what he was supposed to have brought.

"What?" he said.

"Oh, Garp," Cushie said. "Don't you have any *rubbers?*"

He looked apologetically at her. He was only a boy who'd lived his whole life with his mother, and the only rubber he'd seen had been slipped over the doorknob of their apartment in the infirmary annex, probably by a fiendish boy named Meckler—long since graduated and gone on to destroy himself.

Still, he should have known: Garp had heard much conversation of rubbers, of course.

"Come here," Cushie said. She led him to the cannons. "You've never done this, have you?" she asked him. He shook his head, honest to his sheepish core. "Oh, Garp," she said. "If you weren't such an old friend." She smiled at him, but he knew she wouldn't let him do it, now. She pointed into the mouth of the middle cannon. "Look," she said. He looked. A jewel-like sparkle of ground glass, like pebbles he imagined might make up a tropical beach; and something else—not so pleasant. "Rubbers," Cushie told him.

The cannon was crammed with old condoms. Hundreds of prophylactics! A display of arrested reproduction. Like dogs urinating around the borders of their territory, the boys of the

Steering School had left their messes in the mouth of the mammoth cannon guarding the Steering River. The modern world had left its stain upon another historical landmark.

Cushie was getting dressed. "You don't know anything," she teased him, "so what are you going to write about?" He had suspected this would pose a problem for a few years—a kink in his career plans.

He was about to get dressed but she made him lie down so that she could look at him. "You *are* beautiful," she said. "And it's all right." She kissed him.

"I can go *get* some rubbers," he said. "It wouldn't take long, would it? And we could come back."

"My train leaves at five," Cushie said, but she smiled sympathetically.

"I didn't think you had to be back at any special time," Garp said.

"Well, even Dibbs has *some* rules, you know," Cushie said; she sounded hurt by her school's lax reputation. "And besides," she said, "you see Helen. I know you do, don't you?"

"Not like this," he admitted.

"Garp, you shouldn't tell anybody everything," Cushie said.

It was a problem with his writing, too; Mr. Tinch had told him.

"You're too serious, all the time," Cushie said, because for once she was in a position where she could lecture him.

On the river below them an eight-oared shell sleeked through the narrow channel of water remaining in The Gut and rowed toward the Steering boathouse before the tide went out and left them without enough water to get home on.

Then Garp and Cushie saw the golfer. He had come down through the marsh grass on the other side of the river; with his violet madras slacks rolled up above his knees, he waded into the mud flats where the tide had already receded. Ahead of him, on the wetter mud flats, lay his golf ball, perhaps six feet from the edge of the remaining water. Gingerly, the golfer stepped forward, but the mud now rose above his calf; using his golf club for balance, he dipped the shiny head into the muck and swore.

"Harry, come back!" someone called to him. It was his golfing partner, a man dressed with equal vividness, knee-length shorts of a green that no grass ever was—and yellow knee socks. The golfer called Harry grimly stepped closer to his ball. He looked like a rare aquatic bird pursuing its egg in an oil slick.

"Harry, you're going to *sink* in that shit!" his friend warned him. It was then that Garp recognized Harry's partner: the man in green and yellow was Cushie's father, Fat Stew.

"It's a new ball!" Harry yelled; then his left leg disappeared, up to the hip; trying to turn back, Harry lost his balance and sat down. Quickly, he was mired to his waist, his frantic face very red above his powder-blue shirt—bluer than any sky. He waved his club but it slipped out of his hand and sailed into the mud, inches from his ball, impossibly white and forever out of Harry's reach.

"Help!" Harry screamed. But on all fours he was able to move a few feet toward Fat Stew and the safety of shore. "It feels like eels!" he cried. He moved forward on the trunk of his body, using his arms the way a seal on land will use its flippers. An awful *slorp*ing noise pursued him through the mud flats; as if beneath the mud some mouth was gasping to suck him in.

Garp and Cushie stifled their laughter in the bushes. Harry made his last lunge for shore. Stewart Percy, trying to help, stepped on the mud-flats with just one foot and promptly lost a golf shoe and a yellow sock to the suction.

"Ssshhh! And lie *still*." Cushie demanded. They both noticed Garp was erect. "Oh, that's too bad," Cushie whispered, looking sadly at his erection, but when he tried to tug her down in the grass with him, she said, "I don't want babies, Garp. Not even yours. And yours might be a *Jap* baby, you know," Cushie said. "And I surely don't want one of those."

"What?" Garp said. It was one thing not to know about rubbers, but what's this about Jap babies? he wondered.

"Ssshhh," Cushie whispered. "I'm going to give you something to write about."

The furious golfers were already slashing their way through the marsh grass, back to the immaculate fairway, when Cushie's mouth nipped the edge of Garp's tight belly button. Garp was never sure if his actual memory was jolted by that word *Jap*, and if at that moment he truly recalled bleeding in the Percys' house— little Cushie telling her parents that "Bonkie bit Garp" (and the scrutiny the child Garp had undergone in front of the naked Fat Stew). It may have been then that Garp remembered Fat Stew saying he had Jap eyes, and a view of his personal history clicked into perspective; regardless, at this moment Garp resolved to ask his mother for more details than she had offered him up to now. He felt the need to know more than that his father had been a soldier, and so forth. But he also felt Cushie Percy's soft lips on his belly, and when she took him suddenly into her warm mouth, he was very surprised and his sense of resolve was as quickly blown as the rest of him. There under the triple barrels of the Steering family cannons, T.S. Garp was first treated to sex in this relatively safe and nonreproductive manner. Of course, from Cushie's point of view, it was nonreciprocal, too.

They walked back along the Steering River holding hands.

"I want to see you next weekend." Garp told her. He resolved he would not forget the rubbers.

"I know you really love Helen," Cushie said. She probably hated Helen Holm, if she really knew her at all. Helen was such a snob about her brains.

"I still want to see you," Garp said.

"You're nice," Cushie told him, squeezing his hand. "And you're my oldest friend." But they both must have known that you can know someone all your life and never quite be friends.

"Who told you my father was Japanese?" Garp asked her.

"I don't know," Cushie said. "I don't know if he really is, either."

"I don't either," Garp admitted.

"I don't know why you don't ask your mother," Cushie said. But of course he *had* asked, and Jenny was absolutely unwavering from her first and only version. . . .

BUYING STOCK

Denise Duhamel

". . . The use of condoms offers *substantial* protection,
but does not guarantee *total* protection and that
while there is no evidence that deep kissing has
resulted in transfer of the virus, no one can say
that such transmission would be absolutely
impossible." —The Surgeon General, 1987

I know you won't mind if I ask you to put this on.
It's for your protection as well as mine—Wait.
Wait. Here, before we rush into anything
I've bought a condom for each one of your fingers. And here —
just a minute—Open up.
I'll help you put this one on, over your tongue.
I was thinking:
If we leave these two rolled, you can wear them
as patches over your eyes. Partners have been known to cry,
shed tears, bodily fluids, at all this trust, at even the thought
of this closeness.

ON THE NARROW SIDE

Hester Kaplan

IT WAS PARK'S idea to buy condoms together tonight, his surprise, solution, and seduction. I would have been happy for one to simply appear in the dark through man's special magic, the cold lightweight of the foil packet landing in my hand, the rubber unfurling by design. Now, at the glaring, humming drugstore, I'm not even at the condom section before I spot someone who used to work with my husband, she sees me, and it's too late to pretend it hasn't happened. I imagine Park is stealthy behind me on this mission, but incredibly, when I turn around, he's disappeared. I've lost him on a sudden turn or one of his whims.

"Hey, Charlotte," the woman says. A bottle of emerald shampoo bubbles slowly in her hand. "It's good to see you. You look great." Instantly, awkwardness plays over her uncertain face; my husband Will died a year and a half ago, and people still stumble in front of me. She notes my boyishly chopped haircut, my loss of twenty pounds, and my short white dress before she asks, "What are you doing here?"

"Looking for shampoo, too," I lie affably. I can't remember even a hint of her name, though I can picture her laughing with Will on the shaded back steps during a summer party. Will looks pale in my memory, always sneaking away from the sun from the moment I met him, trying to avoid the melanoma that eventually killed him in a matter of winter months.

She leans in close and taps my forearm with her bottle. "We

really miss him, you know." For a moment she squeezes her eyes shut and her lids crease like thin leaves. When she opens them, Park is coming toward us with his full, smooth stride, and I'm surprised when she waves her fingers at him. "Used to live next door," she whispers.

I can tell she is surprised to see Park slip his hand so neatly around my waist. The two of them exchange a light laugh over this coincidence, but I know they are really trying to figure out who exactly the other is to me. She will assume from the easy touching that I'm already sleeping with Park, and in his absolute way, Park will decide she was Will's closest friend, or mine, in any case, someone important. He's said he doesn't like being on the narrow side of things, squeezing onto the wintry sliver that exists after Will. I don't like being there either. Park is not the first man I've dated since Will, but tonight after weeks and weeks, he will be the first man I'll sleep with. He is the turnstile to the rest of my life, and sex is my token to a wider, lusher place.

Very soon, the conversation drops abruptly off the edge and the woman moves to another part of the store, but the unexpected invasion of real life into this furtive scenario means I can't possibly buy condoms here now. I'm suddenly skittish, and when I take a step out of Park's deliberate grasp, he looks confused, and his head tilts towards his shoulder.

"Sorry, I just can't do it *here*," I explain. I want to move ahead, but the mismatch of the pieces of my life has stalled me at the moment.

Before Park can say anything calming or solicitous, I'm out of the drugstore and back in the thumping July evening. I've lived in the same house and neighborhood for eight years, and even though Will's absence is a solid, difficult presence everywhere and in everything—tonight's task, the store, the woman with her shampoo—I've never considered leaving.

"Hi there," Park says, appearing next to me. He's about a foot taller than I am, and sometimes when he speaks, his voice hovers above my head. "You're okay?"

The woman comes out of the store behind us and wordlessly scurries down the block. It's after six, and soon she blends in with others on their way home from work. Park and I have started out early, and already I'm feeling how long the night might be. At this point, I'm ready to go to bed with him and afraid that if we don't get moving soon, I'll lose my nerve and slide back into grief. At the moment though, we're standing still, watching traffic, and the air is smeary with heat.

"I'm fine," I say, and fan my face with my hands. "You should have seen me, Park. I was moving forward with such purpose—it was really impressive—and boom, she steps in my way and throws me off. I should have expected it. After all, this is my neighborhood."

"I guess you know Janet pretty well then." Park waits for me to assure him on this insight into my life. When I don't say anything, he puts on the sunglasses he has hanging from a neon blue rubbery strap around his neck. "I understand how that could be kind of uncomfortable. A minor setback, though."

I'm not sure who's my type anymore, but I'm easily turned on by Park's long legs and forearms, by his graying hair and slight underbite. At thirty-nine, he's single, never married, and still so hopeful about his romantic future—even with me, he's open to all possibilities. He leaves enough time after work to tend to himself thoroughly—to run, to shave, to buy me a small present, to devise this condom plan—before he picks me up at my house. He is a serial dater, too, studiously full of facts and certainties about the way this particularly thorny world works, while I know absolutely nothing about it anymore.

On our fourth time out together, unbidden, and in the pre-dark moment before the movie started, Park presented me with his medical history—clean AIDS test, STD-free, a practitioner of safe sex, monogamous. This information, he claimed, is what people offer these days for safety, as a down payment on love, though it sounded pretty cold and unbeckoning to me. I looked at his legs crossed in crisp jeans, then at my feet which I'd slipped out of sandals and had pressed against the seat in front of me. My skirt had slipped up my parted thighs a few inches, and I wondered why this simple gesture alone wasn't enough anymore. It would have been with Will. I slept with the same man for eight years, I told Park; there were a few UTIs, no pregnancies, we mostly made love on the bed. I threw out my diaphragm the day he died. The bedside drawer is filled with condolence cards. From the indulgent look on Park's face, it was clear I rolled out of a time warp when I rolled out of my marriage. I am a virtual, wandering virgin now.

"Tell me again why we're doing this?" I ask. I want to be convinced, taken along.

"Because buying condoms will be good for us, something important we do together, each step, choosing it, opening it, rolling it on me. I just want you to be comfortable, to feel completely involved."

Park pulls me towards him. His hands feel as big as dinner plates on my shoulders. He is nothing if not persistent in his goal of sleeping with me because he believes it might lead us to love. Before, when I've closed up cold to him, Park has admitted that he doesn't know anything about making love to a thirty-five-year-old widow. Because of my tragedy, he imagines I'm uncharted terrain, and he is a tireless pioneer in this regard. And he's right in a way; sex with him is my last landscape of mourning.

"Think of it as a bonding experience for us, Charlotte, like a really long kiss," he says, "like a night of foreplay."

I could tell him how I don't need to be involved, how I'm willing to go to bed with him with my eyes closed, but I won't. The thing still left undone between us is urgent. And it has to be tonight for both of us, I realize, so I won't deter him from his plan.

"Then let's go some place there isn't a chance we'll see anyone we know," I tell him.

"Sure. That is no problem at all," he assures me, and offers an open, bowing hand to his car across the street. It is a gesture of exaggerated drama and optimism, like tonight.

When I think of Will, he still causes me accidents of distraction; cups slide out of my grasp as though they're greased, I lock my keys in the house once a month. I saw a bone in a bite of fish, ate it anyway, and for minutes, it bridged my windpipe. At work, I sliced my thumb with an X-acto knife and ended up in the emergency room, tended to by a nurse named Park (the sole hetero amongst the gay male nurses, I later learned), who zipped across the smooth floor on a stool with three wheels. I had blood on the front of my yellow silk shirt where I'd held the wound between my breasts as a co-worker drove me to the hospital. Park stayed with me longer than he had to.

Now Will's face is in the soot on the windshield, and I manage to somehow catch my finger in the car door while Park fiddles with something in the trunk amidst his running shoes and tennis rackets. I know it is the worst kind of pain because I can't even feel anything yet, but in the mirror, I can see it already starting to pinch my face and narrow my eyes. The dark hair at the arch of my forehead clings nervously to my skin. When the feeling finally conquers me, I'd really like to scream, put my head between my knees, rock back and forth, and spit out the salty taste in my mouth, but Park is in the car, tuning the radio, and I swallow everything. The prospect of his sympathy at the moment seems more troublingly intimate to me than anything else we'll do tonight, so I sit on my hand to blunt the pain. I feel the throb knocking at the base of my spine.

"You're really going to get a kick out of this place," Park says, and touches my knee as he pulls into traffic. "I was just checking the map. Found us a little short cut, too." He raises his eyebrows suggestively.

"Great," I somehow manage to say. "Let's do it."

Park is the kind of man who likes driving too fast simply because he knows he'll never get a ticket. He's often in his ER scrubs when he's pulled over. That, the box of rubber exam gloves on the back seat, and his hospital ID which he's clipped to the visor, are his immunity from the police. Now he's driving slowly— not only because he's in civilian clothes, his hair gelled to a casual sheen—but because he wants to show me something.

His detour takes us through street after street of ranch houses with glaring picture windows and abandoned outdoor toys. The evening is beginning to turn violet and unreadable. I imagine this is Park's kind of neighborhood, settled and green enough during the day, the sort of place Will and I said we wouldn't end up in, even when we had kids.

Park suddenly drives over a corner because he's allowed the car to wander right as he's looking left, and the front end scrapes over the curb with a rasp of metal on stone. We go bouncing into the empty street.

"I can't believe I just did that," Park says, amazed at himself.

"That was kind of exciting," I laugh. "Can we do it again?"

"I wanted to show you something." The high silvery arch of a lawn sprinkler just reaches us and pings a few drops on the hood, the roof, and my window before it sweeps away again. "See that house across the street?"

"The white one?" Two bicycles lie on their sides in an empty driveway. To me, the house is a blank, and I can't make out any detail, except for a discreet "for sale" sign.

"Yeah, the white one. I've been looking to buy a house for five years," Park says. "I checked it out this morning. I actually liked it a lot."

"Well, since we're here," I suggest, as the sprinkler waves over us again, "we might as well ring one of these doorbells and ask if they can spare a rubber for us. And while we're at it, maybe we could use their tree house or their patio furniture."

At that moment, a security light on the corner of a garage snaps on as a cat strolls by a tended rectangle of lawn. A few seconds later, it goes dark. I imagine the light strobing as Park and I have sex on that soft patch, my heels catching in the grass.

Park has already given me his adult history of love in neat stories, packaged in little boxes of romance. His women sound sensible, the types to announce, right before the cautious business of nineties sex, that they're about to lay down some rules while walking around in underwear and bra. And never in a tree house or a car or on borrowed patio furniture.

But I'm seeing myself as sixteen again. My hot pants are thrown to the still-warm pavement and my shirt is lifted up over my breasts. I don't see the boy on top of me—except as Will—and I don't feel any pleasure my first time. But I feel something better, the greatest sense of possibility in my life from then on. It is this—not the pleasure, but the possibility—after Will, that I need again, why I am here now.

"What do you think of the house?" he asks.

"Or we could do it on that spot of grass," I continue. I don't like that he's brought me here. "We could do it in the back seat right now, and who would see?"

"Did you ever do that?" Park challenges. "Did you ever do it in a tree house? Would you do it in a back yard now? No, I doubt it."

I'm sure he's been having trouble imagining himself in the rooms he walked through earlier in the day, that he's really waiting for a wife and something other than all this driving and circling to begin. Now I've made it impossible for him.

"God, I just feel so fucking old sometimes," he says, and hits the steering wheel. "It used to just be about sex, Charlotte, but it isn't anymore. It's gotten so complicated."

In a few minutes, the solemn air in the car lifts and Park sits up proud in his seat as his Valhalla appears before us. The Condom Hut stands solitary, square, and tiny in the middle of a strip mall's empty lot. Its high pitched roof is made out of stamped yellow metal which barely glows from the lit sign. Otherwise the place is dark.

"I can't believe it's closed, " Park says, and he just sits in front of the drive-through window, staring ahead patiently.

"Guess Thursdays aren't big at the Hut. Are you willing it to open, Park?" I ask. "You look like you're praying. Are you hoping for God to turn on the lights?"

I lean over his lap so I can get a better look at the stacks of boxes lined up behind glass. I read aloud the hand-lettered weekly specials I can just make out, I tell him about the empty cardboard coffee cup on the counter next to a pocket calculator. I point out the blinking red light of the alarm system which emanates from the depth of the hut. I am touched by the idea of people lined up and patient in their cars, squeezing in this last errand of the day, thinking about dinner, walking the dog, having sex. I imagine giggly teenage girls in their fathers' cars, braver than the boys who wait for them. I don't exactly know how Park and I fit in.

"They used to do one-hour processing," he says. "Jumbo prints. That's how I found out about the place, actually. I came to drop off some film." He shrugs a little laugh. "Surprise."

Park leans back on the head rest and stares at the low, fuzzy ceiling of the car. His shirt has come untucked and hangs over his belt so close to my face now as I'm still leaning over him, that I could use my teeth to lift it up. His warmth, smell, and the stirring and stiffening in his lap are overpoweringly familiar to me. I could rest my lips against his belly's skin now, then against his penis, all unplanned and unprotected, and take him in my mouth.

I did this once with Will when we were on the way to see his parents. We weren't married yet—our announcement was the purpose of the endless drive to Florida—and we'd been fighting since we got in the car. Finally, I said I wasn't sure I wanted to be married to someone like him. Will added that the feeling was mutual. The silence over the seven-mile bridge was that long. Will stopped the car in the fisted turnout that doubled back under the shadowed end of the span. Despite what we'd just told each other, I knew we'd be married forever—it's what we wanted, and children, too. But I also understood, as I leaned over him, that the giving up of other men and other lives for me was still bittersweet. My mouth fell easily towards Will and around him. His fingers played under the waistband of my shorts, and cars passed on the bridge above us.

This must be another life then, so if not with my husband ever again, then still in this car. My teeth click against Park's zipper and slowly drag it down. His foot taps on the brake.

"Oh, Charlotte," he sighs when I touch him. The muscles in his leg tense and relax, as though he's responding to the quick rise and fall of my chest. With my eyes shut, I'm dizzy, but I'm not sure if it's from passion or grief—at times, they've felt the same—so I open them again.

"Jesus, what did you do to your finger?" Park's voice is pinched and uncertain.

"Nothing," I say, muffled against him. "Shut your eyes, Park."

He levers me up and lifts my hand off him as though it's crushed. He reaches to turn on the roof light. I'm squinting now and can see that my finger is banded with purple and swollen shiny and stiff. Even I'm scared by the sight; the finger doesn't belong to me.

"What happened?" Park asks, again.

"It isn't a big deal," I say, and turn away. I'm frustrated and embarrassed now, angry at his insistence which has stopped me cold. "I must have banged it or something. I'm always hurting myself, you know that, Park. Just turn off the light, okay? I'm perfectly fine."

But Park knows better from the look of things. Mixed up with his professional concern—he manipulates the digit, as he calls it, angling it back and forth—is a deliberateness I can't place at first.

"Look at it. The hell you just banged it." His voice is too loud in the small space of the car. "Why didn't you say something? We could have gotten you ice at the very least. This must hurt like hell. I just don't understand why you didn't tell me."

"It wasn't on the agenda, Park, it wasn't part of the plan." What kind of man is he to have stopped me? Suddenly, it seems too much that he's a nurse, a giver of care when I don't want any of that, I won't be able to stand it. I draw my hand away from him. "You're off duty now, anyway. I don't need a nurse."

"Agenda." He repeats the word distastefully. "You can give me a blow job but you can't tell me." To further his point, Park rearranges himself and tucks his shirt back in.

"This isn't going to work," I say, finally.

"Before the ER, I used to work in a pediatrics clinic, right after I got my nursing degree. Did I ever tell you?" he asks, and I wonder if he heard what I said. "I really wanted to work with children from the beginning. Anyway, a little girl had a major seizure in one of the examination rooms. My first week on the job, if you can believe it."

I know I'm supposed to offer him words of comfort in this

pause, but I can't locate any, so I poke and push my swollen finger as he did, and sparks of pain shoot up my arm. "I froze up, Charlotte. Couldn't do a goddamn thing I was trained to do. I just stood there like a moron."

Park flips at the sunglasses still around his neck so that they bounce against his chest, and I have to look out the wide window in front of us. In a gift shop, fenced in by a diamond patterned iron gate at this late hour, a light leaks over a cheap window display. A spotlit Osco Drug across the street is festooned with ripped banners announcing its opening weeks ago. Already there is bright graffiti on the wide glass doors. A slight, fuzzy drizzle, though not the real rain we need, has finally started and completes the picture of a totally wasted place. A slow sap of sadness rises in me as Park continues.

"Charlotte? The kid died," Park flails on.

When I shut my eyes, I can see him swimming after a child who already has a chest full of salt water, who is already submerged. It was how I saw myself as Will was dying, how I still saw myself after he was dead. We had been married long enough to know that something bad could happen, but also that it never would or should. I thought I would never get over it, being left alone.

"I was really depressed for a while about everything, I thought I should leave nursing, move, anything. I got addicted to meds, probably drank too much. I spent some time in rehab because I was so messed up. I thought it was my fault, which of course it wasn't, but I *thought* it was, and that's the point."

I am immobilized and silent; Park knows nothing about my own sorrows, not really, and I won't give them up to him, pass them on like photographs. A car drives into the lot, stops to see us bright in the roof light, and then moves on.

"Say something, Charlotte." Park fears he's misstepped here, and his eyebrows meet. "Christ. Anything?"

"I'm sorry, Park. It sounds horrible." In the stall of our crazy condom-buying errand, he'll grasp at pity to reach me if he has to, but I won't trade tragedies; I'll hoard forever Will getting sicker and sicker, still fading away. "You're too patient with me. You deserve better. I'm not as hopeful as you are, I can't offer you anything."

"No, that's wrong. I just want you to know I've gone through some bad stuff, I've been really sad, too, hard to penetrate. This will pass for you, Charlotte, I promise."

Park's lips are painfully dry and I know I will remember his face just like this. I realize suddenly that he's as scared as I am by the prospect of tonight, though for entirely different reasons. Park will persist with me because he believes in the possibility of love, he's staked his life on it. I'll persist because I think I'll die if I don't.

He shakes his head sympathetically at me and finally turns off the roof light. Then he does something so surprising, I gasp; he puts my finger in his mouth and bathes it with his tongue. With the tight tip of my flesh, I can pleasantly feel the highs and lows of his good teeth, big as mountains.

I'm struck by how much of our time together is spent going from one place to another in Park's car. We have covered ground and miles tonight, but now I want to walk.

"Over there. Osco Drug, grand opening," I announce, and point across the street. "Maybe they'll give us a trophy for being their first condom customers."

"I doubt that," Park says, dryly.

He is concerned about leaving his car unwatched in the empty lot, so he drives slowly next to me over the yellow lines and rutted blacktop. I can cross the street, walk through the overgrown, weedy median strip that seems to divide forever, but Park has to pull a U-turn sixty feet ahead. Still in his car at the entrance to the lot, Park looks at me under the overhang of the store and hesitates. It is the first time we've been apart all night, and I'm convinced that in his minute alone, he's decided to drive off and leave me. I'm almost relieved he'll save himself. But when he pulls into a place and turns off the car, I wonder if he wasn't only trying to determine which spot was closest to the door.

Inside, Osco Drug is shiny, customerless and cavernous, with a corrugated roof and tracks of buzzing lights. At the front counter, a fat woman in a pink Osco smock wears a button with a picture of a baby on it. She looks up from her magazine when we pass. Her expression doesn't change at all, but her unwelcoming eyes sweep up and down my body. I find the soft melodies playing above us oddly comforting because I still know the words.

"Well, I can guarantee we won't run into anyone we know here," Park says, as though this has been our only problem all along.

"I don't even know where we are," I add.

We stroll through towering aisles of picnic coolers and economy-sized cans of cheese balls, small appliances and hosiery, dental floss and party supplies. I'm enjoying the wander, but I can tell Park is flagging.

"I think what we want is politely called 'family planning.'" I look up to the directory signs suspended above us. They sway in some mysterious wind.

"I don't know how you can read such small type." Park squints up at the sign, while I've already found what we're looking for. "Maybe I need contacts."

I decide not tell him about the bird perched on one of the steel rafters, tucked in as though resigned to a life of purgatory in Osco Drug. The condom selection is enormous. Before, I might have glanced out of curiosity on my way to batteries or hairbrushes but never stopped to really look. There are rows and rows of little boxes offering the entire range of sensation, protection, color, texture, quantity. On one box, a young couple in argyle sweaters kisses on a beach in the sunset, and I hold it up to Park.

"These two look familiar, don't they?" I ask. "They're probably so old now they don't even fit into their sweaters anymore."

Park examines the box, looks right into their passionate faces. "I think they do commercials," he says and hooks the box back on the metal arm.

"Where do we start?"

Park shrugs, picks up a brand called Rovers, and reads that they offer maximum pleasure with a minimum of effort. When I begin to giggle, he's encouraged and reads awkward English from a box of Silk Kimonos. Soon we're both laughing, red-faced, shushing and bumping each other in a nervous flush of growing embarrassment.

"The thing about condoms," I say to Park as I pick up yet another brand, "is they're great until they break."

"Look for durability then."

Park drapes his arm across my shoulder, my hand grasps his warm forearm because I feel a little drunk and loose. I am helpless when he picks up a brand which promises to glow in the dark, and the tears are streaming down my face. Park laughs so hard, he's wheezing out his words, he rocks from the shoulders, and I feel hopeful about the night for the first time.

But our noise is too much for the vast store and comes bouncing back sharply at us. I know we're sinking into total, blinding inhibition because neither of us can really face what it is we're going to do when we leave. It isn't just about sex. I keep roaring on about the condoms, forcing it even when there isn't anything funny anymore. I am seized with self-consciousness. I think Park sounds like a donkey.

"I'll be right back," he says, His face is very red, his mouth still in a laugh. "Don't go anywhere."

I watch him jog away full of athletic energy to the very far end of the aisle where he stops at the soaps and scented powders we passed earlier. He examines the bars, holding up one after another to the light, then to his nose. He pulses a cloud of bath powder in the air and smells that. Suddenly, I am inert and shivering in my thin dress, a box of condoms clutched in my hand.

A man to my left appears out of nowhere. He is curly-haired and painfully thin, about my age, and the way his madras shirt is tucked carefully into his shorts makes me think someone is waiting for him. He looks like a professor, a little bookish and quick-tempered, and I know what he's doing in this place—hoping for a moment alone. But I am pleased when he gives me an understanding, sheepish smirk and pushes his glasses up his nose. When he squats down to squint at the boxes, his knees crack, but he knows exactly what he's looking for. The small box hides in his hand which he keeps close to his side as he walks away.

He must sense that I'm still staring, because he turns his head. This time, he gives me a decidedly less friendly look, as if to say sex is still something we do in private, we pretend to love alone. Look away.

I see Park approaching me now with a bright, fruity soap in each flat palm. Even now, he is determined to give me a gift of courtship, as though this is some other time, we're other people going somewhere else, and I know I won't sleep with him, tonight or ever.

If sex offers the possibility of love—and we both must still believe this or we wouldn't be here—I'm not ready to give up Will just yet; he was, and still is, all my possibility. I've got a box in my hand as I move down the aisle, away from Park. I hope he'll understand, but at the moment he thinks I'm still full of play and quickens his pace after me.

In a second, I'm running. He runs for a minute after me, then I hear him stop on the linoleum. I know I've passed the small appliance section already, and the picnic coolers. I see the woman in the smock at the front, the wide glass scrawled-on doors, the lot, and Park's car under the brightest light. An alarm follows me out of the store, yawning as it trails me into the street.

I'm not in a place I know, and I don't have any idea which way to head, but I run and run, and then I walk. Somewhere along the way, I've dropped the box. I want to be private with Will for now, even if he is cremated, memorialized, an airy presence in the dark, with me still on this wide, lush median that leads toward home.

CONDOMOLOGY
IN TWELVE EASY LESSONS

Cathryn Alpert

1) Buy a size that fits. Condoms come in a variety of sizes: Large, Extra Large, King Size, Jumbo, Colossal, Mammoth, Gargantuan, Humongous, and John Dillinger.

2) Make sure the size you have selected fits snugly on your penis. Penises come in a variety of sizes: Small, medium, and large.

3) Once you have selected a size that fits, find an appropriate partner to try it out on. Partners can be male or female, depending on your persuasion. If you use enough persuasion, they can be male and female.

4) Don't feel embarrassed when you slip on your condom. Simply pick yourself up off the floor and be more careful the next time.

5) If your condom is lubricated, take precautions not to slime your partner's leg while you fumble to put it on. Statistics show that leg-sliming results in even fewer pregnancies than condom use.

6) If you are nervous about the moment, ask your partner to help you roll the prophylactic onto your penis. Pretend to find this erotic. If he or she giggles, try sliming.

7) If your condom comes in colors such as purple or chartreuse, you are too young to be having sex.

8) If your condom comes in flavors, your partner is too young to be having sex.

9) If your condom is ribbed, give yourself extra points for sensitivity. You won't feel much, but your partner will thank you.

10) Always dispose of used condoms in an appropriate receptacle. The glove compartment of your father's car is not an appropriate receptacle.

11) If your condom accidentally falls off during intercourse, do not panic. Disengage your penis and carefully fish the loose prophylactic from the appropriate orifice. Buy a smaller-sized condom tomorrow—say, gargantuan.

12) If the next-smaller-sized condom falls off during intercourse, look under *Therapists* in the Yellow Pages. Verify that the doctor's office has adequate parking for your Ferrari.

FOR THE RELIEF OF
UNBEARABLE URGES

Nathan Englander

THE BEDS WERE to be separated on nights forbidden to physical intimacy, but Chava Bayla hadn't pushed them together for many months. She flatly refused to sleep anywhere except on her menstrual bed and was, from the start, impervious to her husband's pleading.

"You are pure," Dov Binyamin said to the back of his wife, who—heightening his frustration—slept facing the wall.

"I am impure."

"This is not true, Chava Bayla. It's an impossibility. And I know myself the last time you went to the ritual bath. A woman does not have her thing—"

"Her thing?" Chava said. She laughed, as if she had caught him in a lie, and turned to face the room.

"A woman doesn't menstruate for so long without even a single week of clean days. And a wife does not for so long ignore her husband. It is Shabbos, a double mitzvah tonight—an obligation to make love."

Chava Bayla turned back again to face her wall. She tightened her arms around herself as if in an embrace.

"You are my wife!" Dov Binyamin said.

"That was God's choice, not mine. I might also have been put on this earth as a bar of soap or a kugel. Better," she said, "better it should have been one of those."

• •

That night Dov Binyamin slept curled up on the edge of his bed—as close as he could get to his wife.

After Shabbos, Chava avoided coming into the bedroom for as long as possible. When she finally did enter and found Dov dozing in a chair by the balcony, she went to sleep fully clothed, her sheitel still on the top of her head.

As he nodded forward in the chair, Dov's hat fell to the floor. He woke up, saw his wife, picked up his hat, and, brushing away the dust with his elbow, placed it on the night stand. How beautiful she looked all curled up in her dress. Like a princess enchanted, he thought. Dov pulled the sheet off the top of his bed. He wanted to cover her, to tuck Chava in. Instead he flung the sheet into a corner. He shut off the light, untied his shoes—but did not remove them—and went to sleep on the tile floor beside his wife. Using his arm for a pillow, Dov Binyamin dreamed of a lemon ice his uncle had bought him as a child and of the sound of the airplanes flying overhead at the start of the Yom Kippur War.

Dov Binyamin didn't go to work on Sunday. Folding up his tallis after prayers and fingering the embroidery of the tallis bag, he recalled the day Chava had presented it to him as a wedding gift—the same gift his father had received from his mother, and his father's father before. Dov had marveled at the workmanship, wondered how many hours she had spent with a needle in hand. Now he wondered if she would ever find him worthy of such attentions again. Zipping the prayer shawl inside, Dov Binyamin put the bag under his arm. He carried it with him out of the shul, though he had his own cubby in which to store it inside.

The morning was oppressively hot; a hamsin was settling over Jerusalem. Dov Binyamin was wearing his lightest caftan but in the heat wave it felt as if it were made of the heaviest wool.

Passing a bank of phones, he considered calling work, making some excuse, or even telling the truth. "Shai," he would say, "I am a ghost in my home and wonder who will mend my tallis bag when it is worn." His phone card was in his wallet, which he had forgotten on the dresser, and what did he want to explain to Shai for, who had just come from a Shabbos with his spicy wife and a house full of children.

Dov followed Jaffa Street down to the Old City. Roaming the alleyways always helped calm him. There was comfort in the Jerusalem stone and the walls within walls and the permanence of everything around him. He felt a kinship with history's Jerusalemites, in whose struggles he searched for answers to his own. Lately he felt closer to his biblical heroes than the people with whom he spent his days. King David's desires were far more alive to Dov than the empty problems of Shai and the other men at the furniture store.

Weaving through the Jewish Quarter, he had intended to end up at the Wall, to say Tehillim, and, in his desperate state, scribble a note and stuff it into a crack just like the tourists in their cardboard yarmulkes. Instead, he found himself caught up in the rush inside the Damascus Gate. An old Arab woman was crouched behind a wooden box of cactus fruit. She peeled a sabra with a kitchen knife, allowing a small boy a sample of her product. The child ran off with his mouth open, a stray thorn stuck in his tongue.

Dov Binyamin tightened his hold on the tallis bag and pushed his way through the crowd. He walked back to Mea Shearim along the streets of East Jerusalem. Let them throw stones, he thought. Though no one did. No one even took notice of him except to step out of his way as he rushed to his rebbe's house for some advice.

Meir the Beadle was in the front room, sitting on a plastic chair at a plastic table.

"Don't you have work today?" Meir said, without looking up from the papers that he was shifting from pile to pile. Dov Binyamin ignored the question.

"Is the Rebbe in?"

"He's very busy." Dov Binyamin went over to the kettle, poured himself a mug full of hot water, and stirred in a spoonful of Nescafé.

"How about you don't give me a hard time today?"

"Who's giving a hard time?" Meir said, putting down the papers and getting up from the chair. "I'm just telling you Sunday is busy after a day and a half without work." He knocked at the Rebbe's door and went in. Dov Binyamin made a blessing over his coffee, took a sip, and, being careful not to spill, lowered himself into one of the plastic chairs. The coffee cut the edge off the heat that, like Dov, sat heavy in the room.

The Rebbe leaned forward on his shtender and rocked back and forth as if he were about to topple.

"No, this is no good. Very bad. Not good at all." He pulled back on the lectern and held it in that position. The motion reminded Dov of his dream, of the rumbling of engines and a vase—there had been a blue glass vase—sent to rocking on a shelf. "And you don't want a divorce?"

"I love her, Rebbe. She is my wife."

"And Chava Bayla?"

"She, thank God, has not even raised the subject of separation. She asks nothing of me but to be left alone. And this is where the serpent begins to swallow its tail. The more she rejects me, the more I want to be with her. And the more I want to be with her, the more intent she becomes that I stay away."

"She is testing you."

"Yes. In some way, Rebbe, Chava Bayla is giving to me a test."

Pulling his beard, the Rebbe again put his full weight on the lectern so that the wood creaked. He spoke in a Talmudic sing-song:

"Then you must find the strength to ignore Chava Bayla, until Chava Bayla should come to find you—and you must be strict with yourself. For she will not consider your virtues until she is calm in the knowledge that her choices are her own."

"But I don't have the strength. She is my wife. I miss her. And I am human, too. With human habits. It will be impossible for me not to try and touch her, to try and convince her. Rebbe, forgive me, but God created the world with a certain order to it. I suffer greatly under the urges with which I have been blessed."

"I see," said the Rebbe. "The urges have become great."

"Unbearable. And to be around someone I feel so strongly for, to look and be unable to touch—it is like floating through Heaven in a bubble of Hell."

The Rebbe pulled a chair over to the bookcases that lined his walls. Climbing onto the chair, he steadied himself, then removed a volume from the top shelf. "We must relieve the pressure."

"It is a fine notion. But I fear it's impossible."

"I'm giving you a heter," the Rebbe said. "A special dispensation." He went over to his desk and flipped through the book. He began to scribble on a pad of onionskin paper.

"For what?"

"To see a prostitute."

"Excuse me, Rebbe?"

"Your marriage is at stake, is it not?"

Dov bit at his thumbnail and then rushed the hand, as if it were something shameful, into the pocket of his caftan.

"Yes," he said, a shake entering his voice. "My marriage is a withered limb at my side."

The Rebbe aimed his pencil at Dov.

"One may go to great lengths in the name of achieving peace in the home."

"But a prostitute?" Dov Binyamin asked.

"For the relief of unbearable urges," the Rebbe said. And he tore, like a doctor, the sheet of paper from the pad.

Dov Binyamin drove to Tel-Aviv, the city of sin. There he was convinced he would find plenty of prostitutes. He parked his Fiat on a side street off Dizengoff and walked around town.

Though he was familiar with the city, its social aspects were foreign to him. It was the first leisurely walk he had taken in Tel-Aviv and, fancying himself an anthropologist in a foreign land, he found it all quite interesting. It was usually he who was under scrutiny. Busloads of American tourists scamper through Mea Shearim daily. They buy up the stores and pull tiny cameras from their hip-packs, snapping pictures of real live Hassidim, like the ones from the stories their grandparents told. Next time he would say "Boo!" He laughed at the thought of it. Already he was feeling lighter. Passing a kiosk, he stopped and bought a bag of pizza-flavored Bissli. When he reached the fountain, he sat down on a bench among the aged new-immigrants. They clustered together as if huddled against a biting cold wind that had followed them from their native lands. He stayed there until dark, until the crowd of new-immigrants, like the bud of a flower, began to spread out, to open up, as the old folks filed down the fountain's ramps onto the city streets. They were replaced by young couples and groups of boys and girls who talked to each other from a distance but did not mix. So much like religious children, he thought. In a way we are all the same. Dov Binyamin suddenly felt overwhelmed. He was startled to find himself in Tel-Aviv, already involved in the act of searching out a harlot, instead of home in his chair by the balcony, worrying over whether to take the Rebbe's advice at all.

He walked back to his car. A lone cab driver leaned up against the front door of his Mercedes, smoking. Dov Binyamin approached him, the heat of his feet inside his shoes becoming more oppressive with every step.

"Forgive me," Dov Binyamin said.

The cab driver, his chest hair sticking out of the collar of his T-shirt in tufts, ground out the cigarette and opened the passenger door. "Need a ride, Rabbi?"

"I'm not a rabbi."

"And you don't need a ride?"

Dov Binyamin adjusted his hat. "No. Actually no."

The cab driver lit another cigarette, flourishing his Zippo impressively. Dov took notice, though he was not especially impressed.

"I'm looking for a prostitute."

The cab driver coughed and clasped a hand to his chest.

"Do I look like a prostitute?"

"No, you misunderstand." Dov Binyamin wondered if he should turn and run away. "A female prostitute."

"What's her name?"

"No name. Any name. You are a taxi driver. You must know where are such women." The taxi driver slapped the hood of his car and said, "Ha," which Dov took to be laughter. Another cab pulled up on Dov's other side.

"What's happening?" the second driver called.

"Nothing. The rabbi here wants to know where to find a friend. Thinks it's a cab driver's responsibility to direct him."

"Do we work for the Ministry of Tourism?" the second driver asked.

"I just thought," Dov Binyamin said. His voice was high and cracking. It seemed to elicit pity in the second driver.

"There's a cash machine back on Dizengoff."

"Prostitutes at the bank?" Dov Binyamin said.

"No, not at the bank. But the service isn't free." Dov blushed under his beard. "Up by the train station in Ramat Gan—at the row of bus stops."

"All those pretty ladies aren't waiting for the bus to Haifa." This from the first driver who again slapped the hood of his car and said, "Ha!"

The first time past, he did not stop, driving by the women at high speed and taking the curves around the cement island so that his wheels screeched and he could smell the burning rubber. Dov Binyamin slowed down, trying to maintain control of himself and the car, afraid that he had already drawn too much attention his way. The steering wheel began to vibrate in Dov's shaking hands. The Rebbe had given him permission, had instructed him. Was not the Rebbe's heter valid? This is what Dov Binyamin told his hands but they continued to tremble in protest.

On his second time past, a woman approached the passenger door. She wore a matching shirt and pants. The outfit clung tightly, and Dov could see the full form of her body. Such immodesty! She tapped at the window. Dov Binyamin reached over to roll it down. Flustered, he knocked the gear shift and the car lurched forward. Applying the parking brake, he opened the window the rest of the way.

"Close your lights," she instructed him. "We don't need to be on stage out here."

"Sorry," he said, shutting off the lights. He was comforted by the error, not wanting the woman to think he was the kind of man who employed prostitutes on a regular basis.

"You interested in some action?"

"Me?"

"A shy one," she said. She leaned through the window and Dov

Binyamin looked away from her large breasts. "Is this your first time? Don't worry. I'll be gentle. I know how to treat a black hat."

Dov Binyamin felt the full weight of what he was doing. He was giving a bad name to all Hassidim. It was a sin against God's name. The urge to drive off, to race back to Jerusalem and the silence of his wife, came over Dov Binyamin. He concentrated on his dispensation.

"What would you know from black hats?" he said.

"Plenty," she said. And then, leaning in further, "Actually, you look familiar." Dov Binyamin seized up, only to begin shaking twice as hard. He shifted into first and gave the car some gas. The prostitute barely got clear of the window.

When it seemed as if he wouldn't find a suitable match, a strong-looking young woman stepped out of the darkness.

"Good evening," he said.

She did not answer or ask any questions or smile. She opened the passenger door and sat down.

"What do you think you're doing?"

"Saving you the trouble of driving around like a schoolboy until the sun comes up." She was American. He could hear it. But she spoke beautiful Hebrew, sweet and strong as her step. Dov Binyamin turned on his headlights and again bumped the gear shift so that the car jumped.

"Settle down there, Tiger," she said. "The hard part's over. All the rest of the work is mine."

The room was in an unlicensed hostel. It had its own entrance. There was no furniture other than a double bed, and three singles. The only lamp stood next to the door.

The prostitute sat on the big bed with her legs curled underneath her. She said her name was Devorah.

"Like the prophetess," Dov Binyamin said.

"Exactly," Devorah said. "But I can only see into the immediate future."

"Still, it is a rare gift with which to have been endowed." Dov shifted his weight from foot to foot. He stood next to the large bed unable to bring himself to bend his knees.

"Not really," she said. "All my clients already know what's in store."

She was fiery, this one. And their conversation served to warm up the parts of Dov the heat wave had not touched. The desire that had been building in Dov over the many months filled his body so he was surprised his skin did not burst from the pressure. He tossed his hat onto the opposite single, hoping to appear at ease, as sure of himself as the hairy-chested cab driver with his cigarettes. The hat landed brim side down. Dov's muscles twitched reflexively, though he did not flip it onto its crown.

"Wouldn't you rather make your living as a prophetess?" he asked.

"Of course. Prophesizing's a piece of cake. You don't have to primp all day for it. And it's much easier on the back, no wear and tear. Better for *you*, too. At least you'd leave with something in the morning." She took out one of her earrings, then, as an after-thought, put it back in. "Doesn't matter anyway. No money in it. They pay me to do everything *except* look into the future."

"I'll be the first then," he said, starting to feel almost comfortable. "Tell me what you see."

She closed her eyes and tilted her head so that her lips began to part, this in the style of those who peer into other realms. "I predict that this is the first time you've done such a thing."

"That is not a prophecy. It's a guess." Dov Binyamin cleared his throat and wiggled his toes against the tops of his shoes. "What else do you predict?"

She massaged her temples and held back a naughty grin.

"That you will, for once, get properly laid."

But this was too much for Dov Binyamin. Boiling in the heat and his shame, he fetched his hat.

Devorah took his hand.

"Forgive me," she said, "I didn't mean to be crude."

Her fingers were tan and thin, more delicate than Chava's. How strange it was to see strange fingers against the whiteness of his own.

"Excluding the affections of my mother, blessed be her memory, this is the first time I have been touched by a woman that is not my wife."

She released her grasp and, before he had time to step away, reached out for him again, this time more firmly as if shaking on a deal. Devorah raised herself up and straightened a leg, displayed it for a moment, and then let it dangle over the side of the bed. Dov admired the leg, and the fingers resting against his palm.

"Why are we here together?" she asked—she was not mocking him. Devorah pulled at the hand and he sat at her side.

"To relieve my unbearable urges. So that my wife will be able to love me again."

Devorah raised her eyebrows and pursed her lips.

"You come to me for your wife's sake?"

"Yes."

"You are a very dedicated husband."

She gave him a smile that said, you won't go through with it. The smile lingered, and then he saw that it said something completely different, something irresistible. And he wondered, as a shiver ran from the trunk of his body out to the hand she held, if what they say about American women is true.

Dov walked toward the door, not to leave, but to shut off the lamp.

"One minute," Devorah said, reaching back and removing a

condom from a tiny pocket—no more than a slit in the smooth black fabric of her pants. Dov Binyamin knew what it was and waved it away.

"Am I really your second?" she asked.

Dov heard more in the question than was intended. He heard a flirtation; he heard a woman who treated the act of being second as if it were special. He was sad for her—wondering if she had ever been anyone's first. He did not answer out loud, but instead, nodded, affirming.

Devorah pouted as she decided, the prophylactic held between two fingers like a quarter poised at the mouth of a jukebox. Dov switched off the light and took a half step toward the bed. He stroked at the darkness, moving forward until he found her hair, soft, alive, without any of the worked-over stiffness of Chava's wigs.

"My God," he said, snatching back his hand as if he had been stung. It was too late though. That he already knew. The hunger had flooded his whole self. His heart was swollen with it, pumping so loudly and with such strength it overpowered whatever sense he might have had. For whom then, he wondered, was he putting on, in darkness, such a bashful show? He reached out again and stroked her hair, shaking but sure of his intent. With his other arm, the weaker arm to which he bound every morning his tefillin, the arm closer to the violent force of his heart, he searched for her hand.

Dov found it and took hold of it, first roughly, as if desperate. Then he held it lightly, delicately, as if it was made of blown glass—a goblet from which, with ceremony, he wished to drink. Bringing it toward his mouth, he began to speak.

"It is a sin to spill seed in vain," he said, and Devorah let the condom fall at the sound of his words.

• •

Dov Binyamin was at work on Monday and he was home as usual on Monday night. There was no desire to slip out of the apartment during the long hours when he could not sleep, no temptation, when making a delivery in Ramot, to turn the car in the direction of Tel-Aviv. Dov Binyamin felt, along with a guilt he could not shake, a sense of relief. He knew he could never be with another woman again. And if it were possible to heap on himself all the sexual urges of the past months, if he could undo the single night with the prostitute to restore his unadulterated fidelity, he would have it tenfold. From that night of indulgence he found the strength to wait a lifetime for Chava's attentions—if that need be.

When Chava Bayla entered the dining room, Dov Binyamin would move into the kitchen. When she entered the bedroom, he would close his eyes and feign sleep. He would lie in the dark and silently love his wife. And, never coming to a conclusion, he would rethink the wisdom of the Rebbe's advice. He would picture the hairy arm of the cab driver as he slapped the hood of his taxi. And he would chide himself. Never, never would he accuse his wife of faking impurity, for was it not the greater sin for him to pretend to be pure?

It was only a number of days from that Sunday night that Chava Bayla began to talk to her husband with affection. Soon after, she touched him on the shoulder while handing him a platter of kasha varneshkes. He placed it on the table and ate in silence. As she served dessert, levelesh, his favorite, Dov's guilt took on a physical form. What else could it be? What else but guilt would strike a man so obviously?

It began as a concentrated smoldering that flushed the whole of his body. Quickly intensifying, it left him almost feverish. He would excuse himself from meals and sneak out of bed. At work, frightened and in ever increasing pain, he ran from customers to examine himself in the bathroom. Dov Binyamin knew he was suffering from something more than shame.

But maybe it was a trial, a test of which the Rebbe had not warned him. For as his discomfort increased so did Chava's attentions. On her way out of the shower, she let her towel drop in front of him, stepping away from it as if she hadn't noticed, like some Victorian woman waiting for a gentleman to return her hankie with a bow. She dressed slowly, self-consciously, omitting her undergarments and looking to Dov to remind her. He ignored it all, feeling the weight of his heart—no longer pumping as if to burst, but just as large—the blood stagnant and heavy. Chava began to linger in doorways so that he would be forced to brush against her as he passed. Her passion was torturous to Dov, forced to keep his own hidden inside. Once, without any of the protocol with which they tempered their lives, she came at the subject head-on. "Are you such a small man," she said, "that you must for eternity exact revenge?" He made no answer. It was she who walked away, only to return sweeter and bolder. She became so daring, so desperate, that he wondered if he had ever known the true nature of his wife at all. But he refused, even after repeated advances, to respond to Chava Bayla in bed.

She called to him from the darkness.

"Dovey, please, come out of there. Come lie by me and we'll talk. Just talk. Come Doveleh, join me in bed."

Dov Binyamin stood in the dark in the bathroom. There was some light from the street, enough to make out the toilet and the sink. He heard every word his wife said, and each one tore at him.

He stood before the toilet, holding his penis lightly, mindful of halacha and the laws concerning proper conduct in the lavatory. Trying to relieve himself, to pass water, he suffered to no end.

When he began to urinate, the burning worsened. He looked

down in the half-darkness and imagined he saw flames flickering from his penis.

He recalled the words of the prostitute. For his wife's sake, he thought, as the tears welled up in his eyes. This couldn't possibly be the solution the Rebbe intended. Dov was supposed to be in his wife's embrace, enjoying her caresses, and instead he would get an examination table and a doctor's probing hands.

Dov Binyamin dropped to his knees and rested his head against the coolness of the bowl. Whatever the trial, he couldn't bear it much longer. He had by now earned, he was sure, Chava Bayla's love.

There was a noise, it startled him, it was Chava at the door trying to open it. Dov had locked himself in. The handle turned again, and then Chava spoke to him through the door's frosted glass window.

"Tell me," she said. "Tell me: When did I lose my husband for good?"

Every word a plague.

Dov pressed the lever of the toilet, drowning out Chava Bayla's voice. He let the tears run down his face and took his penis full in his hand.

For Dov Binyamin was on fire inside.

And yet he would not be consumed.

PROTECTION

Gregg Shapiro

My mother kept a squat, yellow jar of Topaz hand
cream, a couple of dog-eared paperback mysteries,
crossword puzzle magazines and a red mechanical
pencil on top of the headboard. My father kept
condoms and some sexy reading material of his own
in the sliding-door compartment of the headboard,
within his reach. I found this stash once, after
detecting the walnut wood door opened a crack.
I carefully turned a page or two of the book with
the missing cover, my hands shiny and slightly
sticky, smelling like my mother's, stopping when
I realized I was leaving greasy, scented fingerprints
on the pages. The foil wrapped discs were only
a minor curiosity, like squeaking bedsprings,
garter belts and the box of Kotex on the floor
in a corner of the bathroom linen closet.

When Billy, a seductive, blond next-door-neighbor
boy, and I discovered how much better we liked each
other, naked and excited, in his parents' bed, with
our TV-hypnotized brothers oblivious in the next room,
I wasn't surprised to find his father kept condoms
in the same place as mine did. I wondered if this
was something they'd been taught at school, by their

fathers, or an older brother. It never even entered
our minds to unwrap the rubber circles, and fill them
with ourselves, with anything other than water or
shaving cream. Back then, we only needed protection
from gossipy whispers of jealous children, the fists
of bullies, older and younger brothers, and parents.

There was only one man who ever penetrated me.
I discovered how to like it, to relax and accept
both the stunning pain and the infinite pleasure
of it. The rhythm, alternately smooth and jagged,
and the icy hot rush of his exaggerated ejaculation.
At the time, when word of the mysterious "gay cancer"
began to make its way into polite dinner party
conversation and small talk, we took precautions
recommended by doctors and those in-the-know. We
taught ourselves to forget what a mouthful of semen
tasted like, how it felt, warm and thick as phlegm
going down. We went to sleep caked in each other's
cum, the sheets crusty, littered with condom wrappers,
the floor a minefield of used and discarded rubbers.

"I want you to come in my mouth," he says, as he unrolls
an extra-thin latex condom over my erection. Well-versed
in the limits of self-control, this was a concept I'd all
but disregarded, having learned to override orgasms, to
come into the air, onto chests and stomachs, thighs, backs
and buttocks. He assures me his teeth will never scratch
the sheath's surface, performing magic with lips, tongue,
 saliva and throat. I look at my penis, chalky, safe
and somewhat discolored by the rubber, flashing back for
a moment, to a time when the only thing a condom prevented

was an unwanted pregnancy. Not entirely foolproof,
somewhat sinful and sacrilegious. In a dream, we fill
thousands of condoms with the helium spirits of the dead
and the unborn. Way over our heads, they become clouds,
rolling like acrobats, muscled with storms. I come in waves.

EXCERPT FROM THE RACHEL PAPERS:
ELEVEN TEN:
THE RACHEL PAPERS,
VOLUME TWO

Martin Amis

HERE COME THE sexy bits. I'm having a hell of a job, all the time whipping from *Conquests and Techniques: A Synthesis* to the Rachel Papers and back again. My files really are in need of thorough reorganization. A good way to spend my twentieth birthday?

I'm sure Norman planned the whole thing. Firstly, he got us all drunk. He poured Rachel out a gin and tonic, insisting that girls never drank anything else, as she well knew, and kept topping it up. Next, he ordered her to ring home and say she was staying to supper. Rachel demurred, until Norman said: 'What's the number? I'll do it.'

Rachel did it.

Then, five minutes later, he said he was taking Jenny *out* to dinner and that there were some sausages in the fridge if we wanted them. He winked at me and Jenny shrugged. As she and Rachel discussed modes of preparing and serving sausages, Norman pointed his great Watney's thumb at a bottle of wine and looked at Rachel with a molten leer.

But I was beginning to feel ridiculous. She didn't want to be here. When we were alone I would apologize, offer to ring her a taxi, make excuses for Norman's intimidating high spirits. As that entrepreneur now took his leave, I winced at his smutty gnomes. 'Be good,' he said, 'and if you can't be good be careful.' Jenny followed him as if bribed to do so.

'Bye,' said Rachel.

It was about seven thirty and the room was darkening. To suspend the moment, underline our aloneness, the street-lights played on the smoke from Rachel's cigarette.

'Can you really stay?'

She nodded.

I poured out more drinks, dutched myself up on neat gin. What's it going to be? I appraised certain gambits—a waste of time; not because of any swinging intensity, but because I felt tired.

'How's DeForest?'

She didn't reply.

I gathered from the female novelists I had been reading (there was a page or two on it downstairs) that the malleable, soft-centre syndrome was no longer considered attractive and that the confident autonomy syndrome was steadily gaining ground.

'Tell me how DeForest is,' I said.

Still no reply. What did she want? Some kind of purer response? It was back to tried and trusted methods.

'There's a stanza in Blake,' I droned, *'Songs of Experience*:

> Love seeketh only self to please,
> To bind another to its delight,
> Joys in another's loss of ease,
> And builds a Hell in Heaven's despite.'

By rights, Rachel should have quoted the complementary stanza, but she probably didn't know it. 'I'm glad you're here,' I said, 'because I've missed you so much. But I still want to get at you although I know how unsatisfying it would be.' I sipped my gin. 'Here's the other stanza:

Love seeketh *not* itself to please,
Nor for itself hath any care,
But for another gives its ease,
And builds a heaven in Hell's despair.'

Rachel received this idiot outpouring with a pathetic nod. (I don't care what anyone says: poetry, if you can bring yourself to recite some, never fails. Like flowers. Give them a posy, speak a verse—and there's nothing they won't do.) Thus:

'I was going to ring you.'

'Were you? But when I rang that Sunday you started going on about cars and roads and things.'

'No, I was going to ring you yesterday.'

There was an appreciative hoarseness in my voice when I asked: 'What for?'

She couldn't or wouldn't answer. I knew anyway. I thought of saying, 'Forgive me, I should like to be alone for a few moments,' but what I in fact said was: 'Hang on—just going to have a pee.'

Within two minutes I had sprayed my armpits, talc-ed my groin, hawked rigorously into the basin, straightened my bedcover, put the fire on, scattered LP covers and left-wing weeklies over the floor, thrown some chalky underpants and a cache of fetid socks actually out of the window, drawn the curtains, removed The Rachel Papers from my desk, and run upstairs again, not panting much.

'Let's . . . let's go downstairs for a bit.'

She stood up and looked at me demandingly. I had nothing appropriate to say, so I went over and kissed her.

'Didn't it work with DeForest, or what?'

'No good.'

My left hand slid off her right buttock and twirled round the neck of the wine bottle.

'Let's go downstairs. Chat about it there.'

But we were diverted by another kiss and soon folded on to the sofa. We talked in one another's arms.

DeForest had more or less fallen apart during the weeks roughly corresponding to the Low. Of course the scatty bitch hadn't *told* him she was coming to stay with me, and he minded her not having told him. Also, though DeForest didn't mention it, Rachel had a hunch that he thought I had banged her on the Friday night. I was flattered to learn that Rachel eventually told him she hadn't banged me—out of the blue. He appeared to believe her, but, five minutes later, burst into tears. Cracked. That was ten days ago. Since then? Smashed up his car twice; crying all the time; stopped working; once came in to Rachel's classroom and dragged her out of it; the headmaster had taken Rachel aside for a talk: the lot. Rachel closed with the not unaffecting low-mimetic remark that she didn't want to make two people miserable so she'd make one person happy, if she could.

'Me?' I asked blankly.

'If you still want me.'

Right then.

As regards structure, comedy has come a long way since Shakespeare, who in his festive conclusions could pair off any old shit and any old fudge-brained slag (see Claudio and Hero in *Much Ado*) and get away with it. But the final kiss no longer symbolizes anything and well-oiled nuptials have ceased to be a plausible image of desire. That kiss is now the beginning of the comic action, not the end that promises another beginning from which the audience is prepared to exclude itself. All right? We have got into the habit of going further and further beyond the happy-ever-more promise: relationships in decay, aftermaths, but with everyone being told a thing or two about themselves, busy learning from their mistakes.

So, in the following phase, with the obstructive elements out of the way (DeForest, Gloria) and the consummation in sight, the comic action would have been due to end, happily. But who is going to believe that any more?

Ready?

Now, as an opener, I decided to try something *rather* ambitious. I rose, poured out drinks, held her eye as we sipped, took her glass away. You really need to be six foot for this, but I gave it a go anyway: knelt on the floor in front of her, reached out and cupped her cheeks, urged her face towards mine . . . No good, not tall enough, she has to buckle inelegantly, breasts on thighs. Rise to a crouch, start work on ears, neck, only occasionally skimming lips across hers. Then, when leg begins to give way, I do not churlishly flatten her on to the sofa nor shoo her downstairs: I pressure her to the floor, half beside half on top of me. (It was bare boards so it must have seemed pretty spontaneous.) Reaching to steady her my hand has grasped her hip; not sober enough to be over-tactical, I let it stay there.

Hardly seemed worth bothering with her breasts. In one movement, her skirt is above her waist, my right leg is between her legs, and my hand floats on her downy stomach. 'Doing' one of her ears I bulged my eyes at the floor. Phase two.

Move my hand over her bronze tights, tracing her hip-bone, circling beneath the overhang of her buttock, shimmer flat-palmed down the back of her legs, U-turning over the knee, meander up her thighs, now dipping between them for a breathless moment, now skirting cheekily round the side. It hovers for a full quarter of a minute, then lands, soft but firm, on her cunt.

Rachel gasped accordingly—but the master's hand was gone, without waiting for a decisive response, to scout the periphery of her tights. And her stomach was so flat and her hip-bones so prominent that I had no problem working my hand down the slack. By way of a diversionary measure (as if she wouldn't notice) I stepped up the tempo of my kisses, harrying the corners of her mouth with reptile tongue. It must be so sexy. How can she bear it?

Meanwhile the hand is creeping on all fours. At the edge of her panties it has a rest, thinks about it, then takes the low road. The whole of me is along with those fingers, spread wide to salute each pore and to absorb the full sweep of her stomach. Mouth toils away absently, on automatic. I nudge her with my right knee and give a startled wheeze as she parts her legs wide. Still, the hand moves down, a hair's breadth, a hair's breadth.

On arrival, it paused to make an interim policy decision. Was now the time for the menace? Had the time come to orchestrate the Lawrentiana? What I really wanted more than anything—yes, what I really wanted more than anything else in the world was a cup of tea and a think. Covertly I looked at Rachel's face: it included clenched eyelids, parted lips, smallish forehead wistfully contoured; but there was no abandonment to be read there.

Nor to be read here. I began to find all this rather alarming. It makes me feel confused, frightened, sad. Because we have come to the heart of the matter, haven't we? This is the outside looking in, the mind moving away from the body, the fear of madness, the squirrel cage. How nice to be able to say: 'We made love, and slept.' Only it wasn't like that; it didn't happen that way. The evidence is before me. (If any respectable doctor got hold of these papers he would have no choice but to cut my head off and send it to a forensic laboratory—and I wouldn't blame him.) I know what it's supposed to be like, I've read my Lawrence. I know also what I felt and thought; I know what that evening was: an aggregate of pleasureless detail, nothing more; an insane, gruelling, blow-by-blow obstacle course. And yet that's what I'm here for tonight. I must be true to myself. Oh God, I thought this was going to be fun. It isn't. I'm sweating here. I'm afraid.

Back on the breakfast-room floor, my fingertips awaited instructions. They had me know that I was dealing with mons hair of the equilateral-triangle variety, the pubic G-string variety, the best, not that of the grizzled scalplock, the tapered sideburn, the balding fist of stubble, fuzz and curls. So, impelled—who knows—by a twinge of genuine curiosity, a mere presence now, the hand went *over* the mound, straining against the pull of her tights and pants, and, once in position, began its slow descent.

This is what I thought. Since Henry Miller's *Tropic* books, of course, it has become difficult to talk sensibly on the question of girls' cunts. (An analogy: young poets like myself are forever taunted by subjects which it is no longer possible to write about in this ironic age: evening skies, good looks, dew, anything at all to do with love, the difference between cosmic reality and how you sometimes feel when you wake up.) I remember I overheard in an Oxford pub one undergraduate—a German, I believe— telling another undergraduate that Swedish girls were okay, he supposed, but 'their conts are too big.' In the same place on a different occasion I talked sex with a pin-cocked Geordie who dedicated himself to the proposition that Oxford girls weren't nearly as good as Geordie girls, the reason being that their cunts were too small. Narcissistic rubbish. Size doesn't matter—unless, that is, you have troubles unknown to the present reviewer.

Which isn't to say that cunts are homogeneous. Now Rachel's was the most pleasing I had ever come across. Not, for her, the wet Brillo-pad, nor the paper-bagful of kedgeree, nor the greasy waistcoat pocket, the gashed vole's stomach, the clump of veins, glands, tubes. No. It was infinitely moist but not wet, exquisitely shaped and yet quite amorphous, all black ink and velvet recessed into pubic hair that resembled my own as a Persian carpet resembles a mat rug. And it was warmer than me; it was, actually, *hot*.

Meanwhile my fingers paddled there, enclosing it with the flat of my hand, entering with one, two fingers, one, two inches, flicking the clitoris. Rachel was quaking and warbling away: however, it seemed right out of context when I pressed my mouth against her ear and (well I never) my sharp erection against her thigh, and said, with a nicely gauged crack in my voice:

'How do you undo this dress?'

Her movements ceased at once. Her eyes opened. 'I'm not on the pill.'

'No, really?' I said.

But then, you see, we did the sort of lyrically zany thing that the under-twenties do fairly often. On Rachel's suggestion, after some tweedy humming and ha-ing from me, we decided that we'd jolly well go up—fuck them all—and *buy* some contraceptives at the late-night chemist in Marble Arch. Nonplussed at first, I soon fell in with the requisite mood. We drank wine, put on coats, and made our whacky way down the square.

Even if we tenderly pooled our money we couldn't afford a taxi—Rachel had to have enough to get back—and besides I thought it more in keeping to take a bus. There was still enough summer about for it not to be really dark, and also you never got beaten up when you were with girls.

It seems improbable now, but on the way there we talked about DeForest's infrequent and ham-cocked performances in bed. (We laughed, too, wholly without malice: an example of prelapsarian high spirits which as of tonight will be another experience unavailable to me.) DeForest's chief, though by no means his only, problem was that he tended to come before either he or Rachel could say—'Jack Robinson'. He would slap on the contraceptive and surge into her with the look of someone who had just remembered that he ought to be doing a terribly important thing elsewhere, like attending his mother's funeral. (I merely annotate Rachel's imitation.) Then he would screw up his freckly face and sink down on top of her, while his prick slithered out as fast as it had slithered in, not to reappear until he had completed a fortnight of stalling, apologizing, rationalizing. I soft-pedalled my amusement through most of this, partly out of real admiration for Rachel's tolerance and lack of embarrassment. But I nearly burst out crying with laughter when she recounted one of DeForest's wheezes to prolong their delight. He took a *history textbook* to bed, which, so the idea was, he would pore over as Rachel shinnied away beneath him; when they were level-pegging, Rachel was to attract her lover's attention in some way, DeForest would hurl *Tudor England* aside, and be granted four or five seconds of impetuous transport before melting into her dream. It didn't work, I need hardly add, though DeForest clocked up a minute on one occasion.

Whether by design or not, this had the effect of making me feel rather cocky. I had come on impact once or twice myself, but only when I couldn't be bothered not to. I would have readjusted my anxiety chart, only I was unable for the moment to think of anything to fill the DeForest's-prick-size slot.

'Have you ever had an orgasm?' I asked, as we got off the bus.

'Never,' said Rachel.

'Just you wait.'

But I soon came up with something. Of course: I had never used a sheath before. With those girls who weren't self-contracepting I had practised coitus interruptus, practising it all over their stomachs or in between the sheet and their bums, depending on locale and whether or not I like them. (There was no definite rule here, yet you were always prompted to go one way or the other.) I was conversant with Durex lore, however, having naturally peed and wanked into them a good deal as a youngster, and

Geoffrey once took me along to score a pack. Further, I had read widely in prophylactic literature. The great things were to squeeze the air out of the tip, lest they burst, and not to put them on inside-out, because then they catapulted off and you opened yourself up to ridicule scrabbling about after them in the dark.

The chemist's was like a chunk of America, a neon labyrinth of bristle and cellophane, ranks and display pyramids of things to minimize your smells, things to soften your hair, bully your spots, reclaim your feet, flush out your ears. We stood in the doorway, shy latecomers to a formal party. The activity and splendour made me feel drunk and empty-stomached. Store detectives, house-wives and dotards cruised the aisles. At the far end a quartet of junkies awaited the return of their forged prescriptions.

'Whereabouts?' I said from the corner of my mouth. Rachel put her hands in her pockets, looping my arm. We moved forward. Only nail-polish remover and badminton rackets seemed to be on sale. Feeling our merriment ebb, I pointed out a not all that unlikely-looking counter. A liberal middle-aged man was in charge of it. What would it really sell? Scabies ointment. Baby powder. Cock-enlarger cream. Dildoes.

'Do you want to come or do you want to wait?'

'I'll come,' she said.

A kooky smile seemed in order.

As a matter of routine, the moment I committed myself to approaching the counter the enlightened-looking man disap-peared beneath it, in favour of a woman with silver hair and a glacial uniform. Oh, come *come*, I wanted to say, you must of course see that this is *too* much like low-brow American fiction.

'Can I help you, young man?' She smiled on cue to reveal oppressively false teeth, dull dying white, the colour of newspa-pers three weeks old.

'I hope so. May I have a packet of contraceptives, please?'

She glanced at Rachel. 'Certainly, sir. Lura, or Penex?'

'The Penex, please, if I may.'

'Twenty-five or thirty pence?'

'Oh, I think the thirty, please, if possible.'

As she turned away I felt Rachel's hand slide through my jacket vents. A fingernail poked my vertebra, making me jerk. Rachel stifled a snort of laughter. The assistant looked up. I met her eye. And my voice was husky when I spoke:

'Better make that a two-pack, lady.'

'I beg your pardon?'

'I'm so sorry. May I have two packets, please?'

'Certainly, sir.'

On the way back I entertained Rachel and kept things going with an account of my own sexual history. Now I had had ten girls. I considered doubling, even squaring, this figure. I ended up halving it. All five, I stressed, had been important and serious relationships. I was sorry, but I had no time for the other kind. Excuse me, but I wasn't interested in purely sexual encounters, thank you, although it was true—one hated to say it—that most of the boys I knew were interested . . . in precious little else—no, perhaps that wasn't fair. Of course I had tried it, more out of curiosity than anything, I supposed. It was odd, but—I don't know—it seemed that a girl's body was . . . empty unless you liked its owner. Sure, the incredibly beautiful girls in these experimental liaisons had got in a bit of a state—what with being so incredibly sexed up at the time. Understandable. (One or two, I didn't mind telling her, had got pretty violent, pretty ugly, about the whole thing.) But I had had just to explain myself, as tactfully as possible. No—hell— they could keep their money; a boy can't fake it.

What was good sex? Well, good sex had nothing to do with

expertise, how many French tricks one knew (how convincingly you munched on each other's stools, etc.). No: if there was affection and enthusiasm, that was enough.

With a heart-beat like a drum-roll I led Rachel down the stairs, past the bathroom, to the bedroom.

It smelled to me of every sock I had taken off, all the earwax I had pasted under its furniture, each bogey I had swiped across its walls, and the bouquets of cheap talc puffed into the air to disguise these. A Low-legacy, perhaps. Or my own stressed senses.

Rachel generously took off her coat while I subdued the lighting by means of a cotton scarf over the desk-lamp. We sat on the floor next to the fire and sipped the wine I had brought down. The pink glow flattered us. It made Rachel look extra Oriental, softening her features, ironing out the nose, giving her eyes a distant luminousness—you wouldn't call it a twinkle exactly. In strong contrast, my face became even more angular and shadowy, more hollow and . . . sinister, my jaw-line more haunting somehow, my mouth—if anything—still more sensual. Let's get it over with, I thought.

'Charles,' said Rachel, 'when I talked about DeForest on the bus, I hope you didn't think I was being callous. I'm really very fond of him. I wasn't just poking fun. It's just that—'

'Ridicule is the only exorcist there is,' I said in a hypnotic voice, 'and laughter the only true deliverance. Don't trick yourself into guilt.—Let's get undressed.'

Balls-aching drivel, unquestionably—and poor tactics, too. One of the troubles with being over-articulate, with having a vocabulary more refined than your emotions, is that every turn in the conversation, every switch of posture, opens up an estate of verbal avenues with a myraid side-turnings and cul-de-sacs—and there are no signposts but your own sincerity and good taste, and

I've never had much of either. All I know is that I can go down any one of them and be welcomed as a returning lord.

Here I had gone and played the sage Frenchie, the crack-barrel *artiste de la chambre*, so 'let's get undressed' had seemed obvious, indeed unavoidable. I had pledged myself to stranded, lean nudity. People really ought to stick together at such a time.

Keeping my body well out of the way, I looked on as Rachel methodically revealed hers. She tugged the elasticized bust of the smock over her head, lowered her tights with an electric crackle, bent and turned to unclip her bra. I was still concealed behind the chair when Rachel went over to the bed, pantied, and slipped between the sheets. Leave them on, for Christ's sake; I needed all the vulgar stimulants I could get. For my knob was knee-high to a grasshopper, the size of a toothpick, as I skipped across the room and fell to a crouch by the side of the bed.

Only her little brown head was visible. I kissed that for a while, knowing from a variety of sources that this will do more for you than any occult caress. The result was satisfactory. My hands, however, were still behaving like prototype hands, marketed before certain snags had been dealt with. So when I introduced one beneath the blankets, I gave it time to warm and settle before sending it down her stomach. Panties? Panties. I threw back the top sheet, my head a whirlpool of notes, directives, memos, hints, pointers, random scribblings.

Foreplay included ear-jobs, bronchitic sweet-nuthins, armpit-play (surprisingly good value in this respect), and a high-jinks of arse and thigh work. The big moment came for Rachel when Charles, the runaway robot, sat up, leaned forward, placed a hand flat on either hip-bone, and literally *peeled* off her panties. As soon as she began to show vunerable self-consciousness (symptomized as usual by raising right knee) I considerately turned my gaze on her face and bunged my fist in the triangle described by thighs and panty-band. Over her knees my reach ran out. Then, in a very superior move, I got hold of an ankle and pulled it towards me, doubling up the legs. In one movement the panties draped her toes. I swung them into the middle of the room.

'Hadn't I better put the thing on now?'

Penex Ultralite come in dull pink flip-top packets of three. On the bed with my back facing Rachel, who stroked it for something to do, I removed a sheath and peered at it: a florin-sized ring of elastic that gathered into an obscene bobble. I undid the elastic with twitchy fingers.

'Won't be a sec.'

But you seemed to need a minimum of three hands to get it on: two to hold it open and one to splint your rig. After thirty seconds my cock was a baby's pinkie and I was trying to put toothpaste back in the tube.

'*Christ* how do you get these things on.' I held it up accusingly. 'Just how, just how are you supposed to get these things *on*.'

Rachel took a look. 'Oh baby,' she said. 'You don't undo it first.'

So it was more necking, strange and perfunctory necking, and more body patrol.

This time, under Rachel's supervision, I held the nozzle daintily between finger and thumb and pulled the greased wafer down with my other hand.

'Oh, I see,' I said.

After all that sweat and goonery, was there any point in trying to find the blighted hair of passion, a whisper of real desire, submerged in that tub of clotted vaginal fluid?

Supported on elbows, I hoisted myself above her and brought a knobbled knee up between hers, through the thighs. Glancing downwards, my rig, in its pink muff, looked unnatural, absurd, like an overdressed Scottie dog. I watched with approval, though, as the knee bore downwards. Then I got to work on ears, neck and throat, and paid elaborate lip-service to her breasts, on the assumption that they were to be found in the immediate vicinity of her hazel-nut nipples.

'Yes,' said Rachel.

Oh, hi. You still here?

Of course. They have breasts, too. Quite slipped my mind. What have I been missing? I bite a nipple experimentally; she wags her head. I brush the other one with my cheek; she grinds her crotch into my knee. I suck on it with stiff lips; her hands grasp my head.

A definite rhythm was now created in her. Time to consolidate it. My hands taking over from my lips, my lips taking over from my knee, I have swooped downwards. It was too dark there (thank God) for me to be able to see what was right in front of my nose, just some kind of glistening pouch, redolent of oysters. A sniper, through those hairy sights, I watched Rachel's jaw tense.

Finally, once her movements had begun to syncopate and turn in on themselves to produce new and altogether different rhythms, and once the secret shudders that have no rhythm started to super-impose themselves on the regular back-and-forth, side-to-side swing of her body . . . then, I wiped my mouth on the napkin of her thighs, and surged upwards, cleverly hooking my elbows round the backs of her knees to bring them along too. My left hand, from underneath, aimed the uncooked sausage on the rele-vant opening. Rachel's head thrown back? Check. Eyes tight, ric-tus smile? Check. And, as I entered, she kissed me, no inhibitions, movingly and democratically partook of her own sour gelatine.

At that point—I swear—I honestly did try to get lost in her responses, to engage her motions, to crawl under the blanket of deliberateness between our bodies. No good. It's far, far too sexy. Real sexual abandonment, for the male, equals orgasm, and therefore he is never allowed to feel it except at the end. It exists, for him, only in indolence or in rape. (If this is so, then, surely, I'm in the clear.)

Seconds away, fusing every nerve in my body, I lurched backwards out of her. Rachel subsided, shaking. Eyes wetted by pain and shock, I placed my head on her breasts. For ninety seconds man and sphincter muscle were locked in combat. I won.

Here we go. An old-school repertoire of minimally sexy positions. Examples: I slung her legs over my shoulders; knelt, bending her almost triple; lay straight as an ironing-board; turned her round, did it from behind, did it from the side; I brought my right leg up, kept my left leg straight—I did the hokey-pokey, in fact. But, again, it is change of position that is sexy, not the position itself, and God forbid that I should feel sexy.

By now my head is lodged dourly between her shoulder and the pillow—no flair, no finessing, just cock to the grindstone. Two times two is four. Three times two, moreover, is six. Stop kissing her mouth, work on ears. Let me come. Stop all movement and kiss her meditatively, in slow motion, so that she differentiates it and realizes what is happening: here I am kissing you. Ninety percent withdrawal, prod her clitoris with my male reproductive organ, feel her contract, smile potently in the half-light. Withdraw to irreducible helmet depth feel her muscles clench and arms tighten pleadingly on my back withdraw till almost out— then—wait—BOOF. She goes stiff then floppy. Pound like an engine, go dog go. Hand on stomach between shuffling webs of public hair, take pressure off, pull legs up too sexy slacken calm down. Fast for three strokes then slow for three then fast. Slow and good, then quick and nasty, then slow and good. Suddenly she shouts, lifts and widens her legs, calls from the end of the world, hands knead my buttocks *don't do that*. Two thirteens twenty-six, three thirteens forty-nine, thirteen twenty-sixes forty-two.

(As regards the physical aspect, by the way, this is all utterly intolerable.) Industrial accidents, pimples, bee-keeping, pus crapping Tampax exams . . . Pick a poet—Because I do not hope to turn the mermaids round from the back singing because I do not hope to keep your hands off me I do not think bloody sheets that they will sing because there can't be anything left I do not hope to turn the pain the pain. Body strung out on a giant whip, the buckled praying mantis soon to be eaten. I grow old I grow old shall I feel her fingernails hear her neigh give me strength O my people affirm before the world no more and deny between the socks not long for the garden where end loves all ten more five more the bathroom in the garden the garden in the desert of drouth, spitting from the mouth the withered apple-seed. (I come now, a token sperm in the rubber nozzle; but that's hardly the point.) Tossed along with the strength of ten men, every second lucid agony, grating thrusts, the crunch of genitals. Then I surfed helplessly on the wave of her climax, pounded and tugged at as it broke by a thousand alien currents. And she came under my dead body.

Rachel's eyes were streaming. She smiled a shamed, apologetic smile. I tried to say something but had breath enough only to mouth it. She saw, though, in the half-light. 'Oh. I love you, too,' she said. . . .

THE CONDOM TREE

Chase Twichell

Pleasure must slip
right through memory's barbed wire,
because sex makes lost things reappear.
This afternoon when I shut my eyes
beneath his body's heavy braille,
I fell through the rosy darkness
all the way back to my tenth year,
the year of the secret
place by the river,
where the old dam spilled
long ropes of water and the froth
chafed the small stones smooth.
I looked up and there it was,
a young maple
still raw in early spring,
and drooping pale
from every reachable branch,
dozens of latex blooms.
I knew what they were,
that the older kids
had hung them there,
but the tree—was it beautiful
caught in that dirty floral light,
or was it an ugly thing?

Beautiful first, and ugly afterward,
when I saw up close
the shriveled human skins?
That must be right,
though in the remembering
its value has been changed again,
and now that flowering
dapples the two of us
with its tendered shadows,
dapples the rumpled bed as it slips
out of the damp present
into our separate pasts.

THE CONDOM

Philip Dacey

He could put it on
with one hand
and in a single
motion so smooth
his woman said

he ought to do that
for a living. People
would pay to see
that, she said.
So he practiced

before the mirror
a whole year
before hitting the
county-fair circuit
where, she was right,

he made enough
to retire on
and after that just
lay around thinking
of a comeback,

of escaping handcuffed
from an oversized one,
a Houdini risking
his life time and again
inside an airtight skin.

EXCERPT FROM
A DISTURBANCE IN ONE PLACE: BROOKLYN *T*S

Binnie Kirshenbaum

IT'S LIKE A string of firecrackers popping off the way they do on Chinese New Year: powPOWpowtityPOWpow, or the rat-a-tat-tat of machine-gun fire. I can almost smell gunpowder. These are the orgasms the hit man gives me, the Al Capone climax, the St. Valentine's Day Massacre. "Snappy the way you Italians do things," I say.

"Hey," the hit man takes offense. "I'm an American. I was born here," although given the circumstances, he can't be too offended.

American. He considers himself American the way an ostrich sticking its head down a hole in the ground considers itself hidden. He clings to this delusion: Brooklyn is a part of the American landscape, like Bay Ridge is Ohio farmland, Flatbush a town with a main street and general store, as if playing stickball in a vacant lot under the el were the same thing as Little League baseball.

I prop myself up on one elbow and study his face. His skin is olive, his lips full, bowed, and his nose—a nose that would be a disaster on a woman—is strong. He has a lot of chest hair.

"So," he gives me a playful slap on the haunch, "how about a cup of coffee? You want?"

"Cawf-fee," I repeat the way he says it, the way he bites on his consonants, emphasizes his *G*s, *D*s, *S*s, and especially his *T*s, adding *T*s even where aren't any, squeezing *T*s into words where they are not written, the way he says *altso* for *also*. He gives words jazz, syncopation. Is it any wonder, then, he gives me orgasms with riffs?

135

He gets up from the bed to make the coffee, but before going to the kitchen he puts on his underwear. Oh, what underwear he has! Magenta briefs and one of these sleeveless T-shirts, ribbed. Underwear that's crude, vulgar, base, unbearably romantic.

"How about you?" he asks. "You want something to put on? A shirt to cover up?" He suggests that next time I come I bring a robe, a housecoat he says, here to hang in his closet.

"No," I tell him. "I'm either dressed or undressed. No fig leaves for me."

I like my body naked. When I put clothes on, it's with the idea of taking them off. I wear dresses held shut by a single snap. A slight tug, an absentminded pull, and any of my dresses will fall open, slide from my shoulders to the floor as breezy as autumn leaves falling from a tree. I am easy to get to.

With this in mind, I never wear shirts with many buttons, tight jeans, pantyhose, shoes that lace, boots, nor use a diaphragm as a method of birth control. I aim to avoid slapstick.

Earlier this evening, when the hit man was over me, kneeling between my legs, he said, "Hold on a second."

I did not want to hold on even if only for a second. Some things can't be delayed without going stale, losing fizzle. He twisted around to the night table, opened the drawer, and fished out a foil packet, a condom. With resignation and pain he sighed, "I guess I better put this on."

This is the truth about using condoms: No one does. At least those of us not part of a high-risk group. Oh, we pretend otherwise, feign social responsibility, claim we use them religiously, but, in fact, we're careless, stupid in our belief that nothing awful can happen.

"I don't know about you," he tore at the foil with his teeth, "but I haven't been with anyone for a while. And that was a pretty long-term thing." Such was the case he pled.

"Skip the condom."

"What?"

"No condom."

"Oh, am I glad you said that. I'm no good with this rubber business," he made it sound as if a condom were an utterly confounding newfangled device he couldn't cope with, the way some people can't cope with fax machines, automated tellers at the bank, or contact lenses.

We went at it then, as if it were before, before the world became such a complicated and dangerous place, when man and woman had no fear of communicable diseases, no self-consciousness, when there was no original sin. We fucked as if we were in Paradise.

I watch him make the espresso, standing at his stove, wearing his magenta briefs, curls of chest hair climbing from the neckline of his sleeveless T-shirt. It's impossible to imagine I will, ever again, get excited, aroused, by Brooks Brothers Pima cotton boxer shorts, Hanes crew neck undershirts.

"You wanT somethinG elTse with the CAWffee?" he asks. "A sweeT, maybe? Or a piece of fruiT?"

Oh, how he sings to me, a siren's song. And I, in a foreign land, am enchanted, seduced by the cadence.

CONDOM

April Lindner

With a soundless rip
the pale balloon rends
and what we perceive as a breakthrough
in our shared love, a tender flood
of trust, as though we could peel back
our skins and give each other
the stripped bouquet of nerves,
this crowning rush of selflessness, is born
of self. It's you I feel for once.
How smoothly the body seduces the mind.
The roots of joy flourish
in our membranes and bellies; much as I crave
your insight, what matters
is how you feed me buckwheat pancakes
with raspberry syrup, how you brush my hair
so hard the bristles
knead my scalp. Some would even say
the love of poetry is nothing
but the coursing of hormones
to the cerebrum. We shiver
but are oddly gladdened by the sight
of shredded latex, by the steep ascent,
the imagined embrace, we can almost feel
a silken beansprout, sightless, sexless,

blanketed by plush, lending weight
to my every breath. Oh happy relapse
like the last bright lungful of deliverance
the drowning are said to inhale, this giving in,
what relief it must be to even
the strongest swimmer, the undertow firm
as a parent, but trustworthy, kind.

SAFETY SPEECH

Cynthia Baughman

"I'M IN ONE of my celibate phases," Lewis had protested in July. His friend Arliss was calling to invite him to a party given by the director of the Women's Studies Program. "Calm, sublimating, productive."

Arliss replied that she felt obligated to her straight friends to force even a broken-down old type like himself into circulation.

"If I go to this thing," Lewis warned her, "I'm just going to make you sit in the corner with me and talk about the masculine voice versus the feminine." He was writing an article on voice-over narration in *nouvelle vague* cinema, and there was a sexual politics angle on which he felt a little shaky. "You can stop me from saying something that will get me in trouble."

"But I like to see you get in trouble," Arliss said sweetly. "It's been one of my chief and regular amusements, lo these many years." Their friendship went back more than two decades, to Berkeley, where she had been a smart young graduate student who spoke with careful wit in his classes and in the same political meetings and reading groups where Lewis and his then-wife Catherine had argued about non-violence and struggled with Marcuse. Now they both had teaching jobs in Cambridge where they had developed a surprisingly intense attachment, alternately sparring and tender. They read each other's manuscripts, went to the movies now and then, and met for lunch almost weekly to gossip about their colleagues, bemoan the latest retrenchments in

141

civil liberties, and haul each other back from the brink of various forms of self-destructive behavior.

"No," said Arliss. "No. You will have rich and rewarding conversations with legions of wonderful women. You will ask them about their work and compliment their outfits; you will compare vacations. You will be generous and charming and warm. For one brief night, you will be very, very nice."

The night of the party was a hot, hot night, and the subdivided Victorian mansion was clotted with vaporous people. Within five minutes Lewis was trying to cajole Arliss out onto a small balcony for a confidential chat. He steered resolutely through the crowd in the living room, squeezed through a sticky porch door, collapsed against the banister, and breathlessly turned only to realize that his friend had been snagged—or had escaped—at the last moment. As the heavy night air cooled him ever so slightly, he leaned against a rail and watched her back there in the lighted room, smiling at the guest of honor, an enormous woman who'd just published a highly-praised social history of makeup. Small, lithe Arliss thrust her hands in the back pockets of her jeans and rocked back and forth in her tiny boots, nodding intensely. Lewis recalled the aftermath of a long-ago dinner party at his house in California. Arliss had stayed to help him and Catherine with the dishes, and Catherine had remarked chattily that one of the women, a rather dramatic painter whom Lewis would eventually sleep with (though none of them knew that then) "looked particularly *made up* this evening." Arliss had replied, "Charlotte has always strained my credibility, but I've never actually considered her a *fictional* character."

Eventually Lewis's eyes wandered away from Arliss and the historian, and over the other gabbing guests—there were dozens and dozens of women in that room. He scanned their sculptural earrings and short skirts and breezy summer haircuts. A slim one in a silky tank top, laughing at her own story, feigned a small collapse against another, and both women staggered a little, clutching at each other in a delightful pantomime of feminine camaraderie. He saw someone else rummage around in her bag for her appointment book and avidly write something down. An address? A bibliographical citation? Her interlocutor reached for the book, and appended a few more lines. Just behind them was the hors d'oeuvres table, and a long-fingered woman dipped one blanched asparagus spear after another into a yellow sauce, and then made her way to a cluster of friends, where she gingerly passed out the dripping things. The room was revealing itself, Lewis realized—as he struggled to hang onto his grumpy mood—as a sea of reception and exchange among highly evolved creatures, rich in appetite and sensibility. For a moment it seemed that he had never seen such a confabulation of interior and exterior vitality: kindness, talents, plumage. They really did look wonderful, these women. And, of course, he was capable of being very, very nice.

Now it was a Monday night in October, and Lewis sat on his sofa in front of his VCR, reluctantly turning down the sound on Jean Vigo's *L'Atalante,* an old French film he was teaching that week. He had just made himself a nifty little supper; he had paper topics to write, and seminar notes to polish, and three letters of recommendation to compose. And one of those terrific women was on the phone.

"I just want to know what happened," said Phoebe Dean.

"I'm not sure what you mean."

"Well, it's been a while since I heard from you. I left a few messages. I don't get it. Are we seeing each other or what?"

"Phoebe," the hostess had announced that night, "is writing this fascinating dissertation on Hollywood films about Vietnam. And she works at the Media Arts Center." Lewis had left the balcony and wound his way into the kitchen looking for something to drink, and that was where the hostess had grabbed him. This Phoebe was tall—more gawky than elegant—with a thrown-together, graduate-studenty look about her, standing awkwardly, wedged between the refrigerator and a Formica counter piled with empties.

"Great topic," said Lewis.

"Lewis does European," said the hostess.

Phoebe claimed to know an article of his on music in Riefenstahl films. "I found it really helpful at a difficult juncture," she said. She punctuated the compliment with a pat on his upper arm which he thought she held one interesting beat too long. They swapped academic gossip for a while, and then Phoebe suggested that they check out the dancing in the next room. After a few minutes in the cramped space, she declared it impossible. Lewis followed her back into the bright kitchen.

"Hollywood is a late interest for me," she informed him, extracting a couple of beers from the refrigerator. "In college I was totally European." And as she prattled on about her intellectual development, Lewis realized that they were alumni of the same institution. "I'm class of," and he lowered his voice and smiled sheepishly, "fifty-five."

The reigning expert on Hollywood films about Vietnam took this coolly, but Lewis was tickled—she was the first Dartmouth woman he had ever met, and he had always wondered what it was like for a girl to go there. She had been an undergraduate in the seventies, she told him, "in the ice age of coeducation." She launched into shocking anecdotes about the hostility and sexism of the male undergraduates. "And half the administration was right in there with them." She described a dean chiming in with a fraternity songfest's adaptation of a fast food chain's jingle: "Fur Burger." And "that meant us."

These salacious, sadistic stories had aroused him slightly. Lewis was attracted by the notion of a woman who belonged in a category which had not existed when he was twenty. Plus she had an animated, intelligent face, if not a particularly pretty one. He suggested that they give the dance floor one more try and was disappointed when he lost her there to a group of buoyant women dancing in a sort of free-form cluster.

He had been astonished two weeks later—"O brave new world!" he actually said to himself—to come home from the library and find on his answering machine a message from "Phoebe Dean, Dartmouth eighty," recounting their meeting and describing a dance band she'd like to check out with him, all in a voice whose self-assurance was charmingly belied by a final rattle and clatter at the end of the message when she had dropped the phone. "And then you dropped the phone," he said to her some days later. She pulled the covers over her head in burlesque mortification.

"You *heard* that? That recorded?"

"I thought it was marvelous. I laughed and laughed. I played it three times." He did not tell her that he had called up Arliss and played the message for her. "Go for it," Arliss had commanded him.

"I deserve some kind of explanation," Phoebe's reproachful voice was saying on the other end of the line.

Lewis punched off the movie on his VCR and it was soundlessly replaced by football. He recalled the fretful look on her face when she had asked, after their first evening out—they had gone dancing— "What do I have to do to get you to kiss me?" At the time he had been charmed by the urgency, the directness of her appeal, and replied, "At this point, not much." He had crossed the room to the ratty armchair where she crouched like a miraculous incarnation of both Miss Muffet and the spider, her long legs sheathed in something skintight and black. Tonight he poked wistfully at his cooling omelette with his free hand and said, "I'm not exactly sure what you mean."

"I've heard so many of your stories. Now I want to hear the one about me."

"No," he said and tried, unhappily, to recall what stories he might have told her. He saw her folded into a corner of this very sofa. Wearing a sleeveless green dress sprigged with cartoonish black wristwatches. "It's a pun," she had explained, fanning out the skirt. "Black watch." She had kicked off her sandals, and it looked like her dusty feet were smudging his upholstery, and that had been okay with him. He was splayed across the other end of the sofa, with his shirt half unbuttoned and a drink in his hand, in a goofy, erotic, expansive mood. Talk talk talk. About Julia's illegal abortion. That had fascinated her in a grisly kind of way. He had recapped his and Catherine's disastrous experiments with open marriage in the late sixties when he was still at Berkeley. He remembered the bemused expression on Phoebe's face when he recounted buying a "marriage manual" sometime during the Eisenhower years, and learning oral sex. "We felt very daring," he'd confided. "Very avant-garde." She had said, "This certainly is educational—oral history," and they had laughed at her bad joke. She had sharp, crooked teeth, and her gums showed when she laughed. He had thought how much prettier Catherine had been at that age, awkward, and unexpectedly pregnant, self-conscious-ly arranging herself into the diagrammed positions, and gently adjusting his limbs.

"You seeing somebody else?" the telephone Phoebe prompted him tonight.

A sweatshirt of Gillian's lay puddled on his coffee table. Lewis placed one socked foot on it and felt mildly consoled, connected with a sensible, optimistic person who always had several cheerful orgasms before she had to go home and pay her babysitter. Tonight Gillian and her daughter were shopping for a Halloween costume. "She wants to be Madonna," Gillian had said tolerantly. "We are looking for a black lace bra in a size twenty-three quadruple A." When Gillian held him in her freckled, exercised arms he felt collected, salvaged. "You look like this great beached whale that I want to drag back into open water," she had told him, standing by his bed, fastening her bracelets. "In the few hours granted the working mother for that kind of endeavor." Gillian was a fundraiser for the Aquarium and frequently spoke in terms of fish and projects. She and her daughter were handsome redheads who called each other "Ginger," though no one else was allowed to.

Lewis said to Phoebe, "I'm sorry things didn't work out between us. But honestly. It was just one of those things. Most things are." The phone felt very heavy, and his dinner was looking congealed.

After a few more rounds Phoebe finally said, "I left my Motown tape in your car."

"I'll get it back to you."

"Well then. I suppose I ought to bid you goodbye. I wish you well."

Bid you goodbye! Wish you well! Who the hell was this? Bette Davis?

But Lewis was not a callous person—he had not embarked on the affair casually, knowing that it would end badly, or even that it would end at all. He was not the kind of guy who deliberately indulged in brief, shallow liaisons. He had, in fact, prepared himself to be dropped by Phoebe—she'd struck him as practiced and impulsive, and she seemed to have asked him out on a whim, in some kind of wild mood. She had certainly not seemed poised to fall in love, or whatever it was that had happened to her. Some pathetic father thing, probably. If he were being perfectly honest.

Tonight she had demanded that he account for the waning of his interest. But Lewis assumed that waning was the sad rule. Waxing was the blessed exception. "I've told you how things stand," he had said. "What more could you possibly want to know?"

"I am interested in my effect on people."

"This makes me very uncomfortable." It was embarrassing and painful. He didn't see how her effect on him was any of her business.

"Maybe it's a generational thing," she had said. "We like to talk about our experience now. We pay attention to our emotional lives. The personal is not only the political. It's also the intellectual."

"Don't talk to me like you're the representative of some sexual/emotional avant-garde."

"I just want to be someone on whom nothing is lost."

"I don't like being handed a subpoena."

The guilt she induced stuck with him all evening. It was unfair.

As he lay in bed that night, with five essay questions on early European film tucked into his briefcase alongside several misleading accounts of the mediocre accomplishments of talentless, tin-eared graduate students, this unfair person rose up, clamorous and insinuating. Her scrawny, imperfect form thrust aside Vigo's ghostly long shot of a bride on the deck of a canal barge, and light-drenched images of strong-limbed young men in numbered jerseys, chugging across enameled grass, tumbling and rolling resiliently, springing up undamaged.

"You," she had said to him with reluctant admiration, ruffling the hair on his shins. "You are my Dartmouth karma." She had knelt beside him on this bed, passing her hand lightly over his flesh, like someone idly brushing the sand on a beach.

"Explain." He had plumped up a pillow and settled back to watch her playful, reflective face.

"I hated it there. I hated the Winter Carnival, the fraternities, the big noisy boys, and the plastic cups all over the place on Sunday morning. I *really* hated seeing the big bruiser football team boys trotting into their private dining room to devour their scholarship steaks and testosterone sauce. I lived near the stadium and could never study at home on Saturdays in the fall, they made so much noise. Their horns, their stupid cheers. The big alumni cars and their useless wives mixing cocktails." She had shrugged and smiled. "Lucky for me, I managed to find these delicate, sweet, articulate, sensitive, alienated boys. Really nice literary boys. Boys studying philosophy and making sculpture. I never so much as ate dinner with one of those dreadful jock boys. You know the only time I ever was in a fraternity?"

"When?" he asked. Her hand had fallen still on his calf. One of her nipples seemed slightly walleyed.

"My freshman year, this girl I was in love with all through high school, who had gone to Yale, drove up with some friends for the Yale game. We went to this fraternity party together, with these idiots who gave her a ride."

"You went as a couple?" The idea intrigued him. Two studious, artistic girls standing entwined, drinking rank beer, and making disgusted, discerning remarks in bold voices, in a parlor where he might have felt up Catherine twenty years earlier.

"Yeah, sure," she said. Her countenance was unreadable, but her tone was superior and slightly contemptuous. "And then, ten years later, what do I do, but start messing around with a fucking Dartmouth football player." She lightly slapped his thigh. "This enormous, hairy, manly, Dartmouth football player. Plus he's from the fucking *fifties*. This class of nineteen fifty-five football player. God knows what you did to women back then." She shuddered deliberately and looked like someone had pulled the plug on her face. He remembered squatting outside the bathroom of Alpha Phi, listening to retching, whimpers, and running water, as his friend Dougie Fugate murmured, "Come on baby, it'll be okay. Come on now. Let's go get some breakfast. Nobody's coming near you."

He had held out his hand to Phoebe. "I trust you don't find the experience as loathsome as you expected."

"The jury," she had said, flopping onto her stomach beside him and nuzzling his neck, "is still out."

Lewis woke to the cool October morning feeling pestered and apologetic. It took him a moment to remember that he was fully prepared for class, and that his paper topics and letters were in his briefcase. His mood was courtesy of Phoebe. Oh, it was depressing, it was costly, to reject someone's affection. As he angled his jaw to give his sagging skin a framework over which he could shave, he felt vain and foolish. He was on his way to becoming an old man; his curly hair had grown thin and wiry; he fluffed it up to hide a bald spot. And he had hurt a vulnerable young woman. Who did he think he was?

He smiled at himself in the mirror and rubbed his bare chest. Its solidity comforted him.

He lived in a turn-of-the-century Gothic high-school building which had been transformed into a mall of trendy specialty shops topped by three floors of offices and apartments. The two main entrances were ornate granite archways topped by keystones, one carved Boys and the other Girls. When he passed in or out (usually under Boys), especially on crisp, back-to-school autumn days like this one, he imagined the two segregated lines of befrocked and knickered adolescents, eyeing or ignoring each other. On his long, pleasant walk to campus he passed a couple of students from his lecture course—a rangy boy wearing a dead man's coat and carrying a lush leather bag, and a girl tidily contained in a buttery aviator jacket and crested with an expensive explosion of hair. "Hi," the girl said. "Professor," nodded the boy. So many college students looked so rich these days. Such perfectly confident, complete little beings.

He had never slept with a student. He was proud of that, at least.

His department secretary liked him. She waved from the phone as he entered the office, and he flapped his paper topics and mimed gratitude as he dropped them in the duplication basket. He gathered his mail for reading between office-hour customers and settled at his desk with his door cracked cordially open. Outside his first floor window, a bicycle rack attracted a noisy crew. Tomorrow's leaders clattered in and out of it all day, banging their locks and chains, and hailing the mutts that loafed and skirmished around the door of the building, while their negligent owners improved themselves inside. He could hear a girl yelling "I'm psyched, I'm psyched," while another one boomed "All *right*."

A pink While-You-Were-Out slip informed him that Catherine had called at nine and would call back at eleven. Even though their divorce had been Catherine's idea, she preferred calling him at the office to calling him at home because she dreaded finding another woman there—sometimes this unresolved jealousy made Lewis wonder how competent a therapist Catherine could be. Catherine still lived in Berkeley. Her genial, flaky husband, Paul, who was also a therapist, called Lewis "my main man," wore dashikis on holidays, and greeted Lewis and Catherine's son

Luther with soul handshakes, even though they were both white people. Luther played drums for an insolvent punk band called Milk Carton Kids, and lived in a warehouse, doing all the worst drugs. Lewis and Catherine spent a lot of time on the phone wondering what to try next.

His mail yielded university press advertisements, a divestment rally announcement, a memo on campus recycling, a packet of offprints of an article he'd written on paranoiac films from the cold war period—published with his photographs and captions maddeningly scrambled—and a blank envelope enclosing a copy of *Steal This Book*, which Lewis had forgotten lending to Phoebe after she'd unearthed it in his study. "I considered it" was written on a piece of computer scrap wrapped around the book. The girl must have delivered it personally, on her way to her office that morning. He wondered if she had hoped to run into him, or if she had figured that the prompt return hot on the heels of last night's valedictory phone call would sting him, or if ridding herself of the book was a relatively healthy act of closure, which he should greet with relief. He imagined her gangly, disheveled form darting into the mailroom and snooping around, poking through the letters in his box.

He was flipping through Abbie Hoffman's book, chuckling, relishing it anew, when an engineering major from his survey course showed up to talk about her paper. She wanted to compare Murnau's *Sunrise*, which he had screened two weeks ago, with this week's film, *L'Atalante*. "In both of them this couple almost splits up but then they get back together," she said eagerly.

"Yes, that's true. There's a plot similarity." He watched her write down "PLOT" and underline it twice. "And where do you want to go after that observation?"

"Well, I think it's interesting." She seemed genuinely excited. It was nice when science students were touched by a humanities course. Except when you pictured them ten years from now, better able—thanks to you—to relax at the movies after spending the day designing the weapons system that would vaporize your grandchildren.

"It *is* interesting. Have you noted any other interesting similarities?"

The girl thought for a moment. "Water. Boats."

"True. Could you generalize about the function of water and boats in these two films?"

She smiled sheepishly and absently dotted her cheek with her pen.

"Well, do they lead anyplace in particular?"

"It's a canal barge in *L'Atalante*. In the other one it's just this little rowboat."

"Right," he said. "But where do the characters end up when they ride these boats?"

"In the city!" She wrote that down.

Lewis talked patiently with the future engineer about what she might do with her material. In high school it was okay to just analyze two things and show how they were different or similar, but in college the comparison had to lead to evidence for some larger argument. That seemed to come as bad news, and despite his best efforts to be encouraging and instructive, the girl got up to leave deflated and confused. Then she stopped at the door and kicked cautiously against the jamb with one sneaker. "I have a question."

"Yes."

"You know the scene where the guy's in bed, after his wife's gone?"

"Mm-hmm."

"What do the spots mean?"

"That's a very good question. It is a famous shot." It was an amazing sequence. The separated newlyweds rest fitfully in lonely beds—the man in the hold of his barge, and the woman in an urban flophouse. Images of water and the face of the other—the face of the beloved—are superimposed on the faces of each of the lovers. Leopard-spot shadows play over the two estranged bodies, giving their skin an astonishing tactile quality. It is as if they are breaking out in a rash, dappled with their own desire for each other. The man, tossing and turning, rubs the hair of his armpit, and it is clear that he is dreaming of his wife, imagining that he is caressing her hair. Perhaps her pubic hair.

"I love your body," Phoebe had said. She lay propped on one elbow, wrapped in a sheet, and trailing her fingers up and down his arm, lightly tickling his armpit, while he dozed naked on his back.

"My body likes you" was his customary response.

Lewis asked his student what she thought about those spots.

She tugged on the zipper pull of her jacket. "I didn't get it. Are they supposed to be real? Were those guys dreaming them?"

"That's an excellent question," he said. "Maybe you could kick off class tomorrow by asking it." He would rather not get into that rash, that hair, here and now.

"Sure," said the student. "*Mañana*." She executed a pleased little salute. One skimpy compliment could turn a baffled, sneaker-scuffing, backpack-toter into a raffish cosmopolitan.

A "C" student from the same class, who had missed the last two quizzes, ambled in. He was there to fish for makeups, with a story about a suicidal roommate. "It's been, like, you can't leave him alone," the kid said dramatically. "I go out to the library and I come back and he's in the bathtub trying to get the razor blades out of a Track II cartridge." Lewis noted the Frisbee sticking out of the kid's knapsack, suspected that he was a con artist, and told him to come back after talking with psychological services and the dean. "They should know what's happening with your roommate. And you need support," he said with his kindliest air.

The kid said "Right," and left sulking.

At ten of eleven Catherine called. "Between patients," she said, and she had some rough news. One of the Milk Carton Kids had taken Luther to the emergency room the night before, after he had lain comatose for six hours in the freight elevator of the warehouse. Now he was ambulatory and seemed fine. But maybe the time had come for some kind of residential treatment program? She and Paul were looking into it. They might need Lewis to sign something.

"Jesus," said Lewis. "You should have called me last night."

"I tried," Catherine said with a hint of reproach. "Your line was busy."

Lewis's son Luther had been one of those babies who cried a lot. The doctor said there was nothing the matter: some kids were just criers. "It's probably a kind of exercise they need." But it had been wrenching to listen to his howls and extrapolate from the terrible sounds all manner of anguish and fear and be helpless to comfort or explain. On top of that, Luther had also been a baby who wouldn't take a bottle. Catherine would stock the refrigerator with slippery little bags of breast milk, and when she went out on her own—to one of her umpteen groups or a class—Lewis would empty the flopping pouch into the bottle, warm it, and hold the nipple over his child's yowling mouth. He would squeeze a few drops onto the bright tongue; he would sprinkle his own finger and rub it over the slick ridge of baby gums. But Luther would never close his little lips and suck. Sometimes he would fall asleep, tears in the creases around his eyes, the folds of his neck damp with the sweat of his exhaustion. Lewis would just watch him then, grateful, and afraid to move, afraid to reach for a book or bend over the paper. He would talk to him, quietly, asking questions about his mysterious infant world. "Are you dreaming now? Do you like sleeping in your daddy's arms? Does my boy feel secure?" Sometimes Luther did look as if he felt secure; the tears would dry, and the tired little face would begin to look peaceful and blessed. But the minute Catherine waltzed in—with some jolly, knowing friend of hers, perhaps—the child would stir to alertness and whimper for his mother. "Is my baby hungry?" Catherine would say. "My baby is so hungry," she would sing as Luther settled at her breast. "Your day will come, Dad," the friend would promise Lewis in that tone of indulgent consolation with which women tease ego-wounded men. And Catherine would stroke Luther's cheek and coo, "Yes, yes. Mother will be all forgotten."

Lewis protested to her now, "I called him last week and he sounded fine. All excited about some van they were buying. I sent him a check."

"The singer drove that van into a parked car while Luther was at the hospital."

"Jesus. Maybe I should try to get him to move out here."

"I really think he needs something local."

"It might be good for him—" Lewis floundered a little, "getting away."

"Sweetheart," Catherine said firmly, "he has a life going on here. The Kids are beginning to get some work, a little bit of a reputation. Whatever happens, he should stay in touch with that." She promised to keep Lewis posted, and then asked what was going on with him. Lewis expressed general grumpy exhaustion, and complained about his flubbed offprints. He resisted an impulse to unburden himself about last night's phone call and his disturbed sleep. Catherine relished hearing about any sexual relationship of his that went badly, but confessions of guilt or anxiety always launched her into therapist lingo, and it made him feel lonely and estranged when she talked to him that way. He hadn't told her about Gillian yet: he wasn't ready to be pumped for details, to receive Catherine's strained and cautious felicitations.

After Catherine hung up, Lewis dialed the Milk Carton Kids' warehouse and an answering machine clicked on and began playing some discordant, undisciplined music which he figured was probably theirs. A voice he didn't recognize broke in, saying in an aggressive staccato, "Are *you* talking to *me*? Are *you* talking to *me*?" Lewis left a message asking his son to call him collect, at home or at work, whenever he got in. He looked up the number of the student with the probably fake suicidal roommate and called him. A different boy answered the phone, with a vigorous "Yo." Lewis left a message for his student asking him to call.

As Lewis hung up the phone, a pallid graduate student appeared at his door, toting a nifty lap-top computer. He was there to weasel out of one of the languages required for the Ph.D. He cited extensive undergraduate work in FORTRAN. "Certainly it's a language," he insisted. "There are natural languages and there are artificial languages. Programming languages employ a sophisticated grammar and vocabulary." He unfolded his lap-top and typed out a mess of numbers, bars, asterisks, brackets, and stunted quasi-words in capital letters. He planted the computer on Lewis's desk and turned the screen towards him with a flourish. "I can read this," he said. "Fluently." He rested his sparsely bristled chin on the top edge of the screen and asked eagerly, "Shall I?"

"Later," Lewis said.

"Philosophy and Math accept programming languages," the student said, "would you like to see their procedural guides?" After making a few obvious points about the relevance of particular languages to particular disciplines, Lewis told him that he would take the matter up with other members of the department. After the kid left, he found himself dialing Luther's number again and listening, with more appreciation this time, to the music on his machine. He hung up and called once more, and this time he felt himself anticipating a particular crash which sounded, gratifyingly, just where he expected it. Thank god *his* son was not an officious prig or a lying little weasel. No. His son was bold and wild, and he stood in the winds of the world and took them in the face. Luther was a musician. An artist. Lewis longed to see his bulky, handsome boy standing before him in all his tattered gear—his leather wristbands, his menacing boots, his tinkling chains.

Lewis was meeting Arliss for lunch, just off campus, in an Indian restaurant where the mournful, deep-eyed waiters and the whiny sitar music matched his mood. Gillian was not available at lunchtime—she went swimming in a hotel pool near the Aquarium—but if she were, she would have been the wrong person for Lewis today. It took a lot out of you, all the self-revelation and self-protection at the beginning of a relationship: unveiling your talents and taking your bows; keeping your bad habits, your chronic meannesses, your characteristic ways of being a disappointment a secret for as long as you possibly could. Lewis was in the mood for a friend who had no illusions, but who liked him anyway, who got from him exactly what she wanted. Arliss had said just that to him once when she was nursing a broken heart: "I was thinking this morning," she had said, "that I have with you exactly the relationship I want to have with you. You give me just what I want you to give me, and I think you feel the same: you don't make me feel like I'm disappointing you—holding out—not giving enough. Neither one of us wants more or less. How often in life can you say that?"

She was there when he arrived, dressed entirely in the grey-to-black spectrum which she favored, sipping a yogurt concoction, and making marginal notes in a journal of Marxist art criticism.

He bumbled into the chair opposite her, jarring the table so that her water splashed on the purple binding of her journal. She dabbed it with a napkin, looked up, and regarded him inscrutably from behind her red plastic glasses. Something about her small-ness, her lesbian self-containment—her physical imperviousness to him—often made Lewis feel gross and self-revealing around her—a bearer of too much body, a welter of sexual symptoms. He wondered what it would be like to be her rival for some woman's affections.

"A bad morning?" she ventured.

Arliss talked sympathetically with him about Luther, even offering to cover a few classes if Lewis wanted to fly out west. She reminisced about the godawful things she had done as a kid, and noted that she didn't regret any of them: "Did I ever tell you about my weekend with the fashion designer and her husband, when I was seventeen?"

"A glamorous alumna of your high school or something?"

"I should dig out the profile I wrote for the school paper: 'On the Cutting Edge.' And then she came to speak in assembly and I introduced her. God I was cool."

Arliss rippled her shoulders gracefully, reached across the table, and lightly stroked his wrist with her tiny fingers. They were cold and wet from holding her drink, and he flinched a little. She with-drew her hand. "No matter what, you are always a little defended around me, aren't you?"

"Just worn to a nub. I had this awful, sleepless night."

"Do you want to talk to your friend? Your very best pal." In less tender moods she referred to herself as "the only woman you've never fucked over."

Lewis recounted last night's phone call. "This was almost two months ago. And she's hounding me."

"You're being melodramatic," Arliss said. "You fancy yourself

159

stuck in *Fatal Attraction*." She rummaged in a basket of exotic stuffed and fried breads.

"You know I'd never have the nerve to say this to anyone but you, but I think that movie was on to something."

"I'm all ears." Arliss relished his willingness to incriminate himself around her. "Your endearing yen for reproval and absolution," she called it. She pushed the bread basket towards him and he fingered its splintery rim.

"It seems to me that—in an insidious, distorted way, of course—*Fatal Attraction* captured a real moment in our socio-sexual history. Women have learned to be sexually aggressive—it's great, okay, no arguments here—they call people up, they make the first move. But then they can't follow through. The thing flops, and they start acting all hurt, like they were seduced. Misled. Betrayed. Suddenly we're in radio song land, and yours truly is a brute and a cad who willfully picked out Little Miss I've-Been-Cheated-Been-Mistreated as his personal victim."

"Hmm." Arliss nibbled at a puffy biscuit with tiny smiling lips.

Lewis probed his ground lamb. "Maybe I should teach it next year. You always give me ideas. I'm doing *Virus* this afternoon." *A Virus Has No Morals*. It was a funny, complicated, German film about AIDS which Arliss had taken him to in August.

"I wish I could be there," Arliss said, bemusement puckering her lips.

The film's basic narrative line concerned the unsympathetic response of a cherubic classical musician to the illness of his bath-house-owner lover. It was intercut with a confusing subplot about a predatory woman with a penchant for bisexual men, and with lurid, disturbing vaudevillian sequences: a transvestite nurse quintet sang an instructional safe sex anthem. A monstrously self-absorbed mother chatted superficially with her stricken son, oblivious to his lesions and pallor. A smug research scientist dumped test tubes containing four different body fluids into a small tank and dipped two dildoes, one sheathed in a condom and one bare, into the brew. Gloating, she watched the unprotected dildo bubble and steam, and then triumphantly exhibited it to the audience, a half-dissolved, drooping stump.

A student filmmaker, who was clearly out of his element in Lewis's seminar room full of critics, presented an enthusiastic and touching assessment of the contribution this film made to "our struggle."

Then a sophisticated theorist wittily analyzed the misogyny pervading the film: "He scapegoats women. He displaces blame from culpable institutions onto a female sexuality which is presented as resentful and voracious." She threw in a few ad lib remarks about who counted as "us" in "our struggle."

The filmmaker obviously felt outshone and personally attacked, but lacked the rhetorical wherewithal to respond effectively. A few students attempted to diffuse the tension with neutral, off-the-track comments about the *mise-en-scène* and the cast.

Lewis felt compelled to refocus discussion on the question of misogyny, while reviving the filmmaker's best points about the political efficacy of the film. "Ben," he said to the intimidated young man, "do you think it's possible to bracket Helen's criticisms, and preserve your sense of the film's usefulness? Or might you incorporate her points into a more global reading?" Lewis smiled conspiratorially: he was passing on trade secrets and wanted his students to realize that. "Of course you can always try arguing that a film doesn't just instantiate its fantasies—it critiques them. You know: 'It's not *violent*—it's *about* violence.'"

"I'd like to look at the first heterosexual seduction scene," the theory student said, "okay?"

Lewis turned on the video monitor and slipped in the cassette while someone dimmed the lights. He fast-forwarded to a scene where a woman in black satin underwear, garters and heels sits on the stomach of a bisexual man.

"He is clearly presented as her victim," said the theorist. "She's a vampire."

While the scene played, Lewis stole glances at the rapt, discomfited faces of his students. Some of them took notes. Others nodded, or signaled each other at key moments. One face was squinched into a sustained wince. Lewis shifted uneasily in the dinky, unyielding classroom chair. The movie conjured up unpleasant scenes from his brief affair with Phoebe. That first night, after they had kissed for a while (she had drawn him into her armchair with twining limbs), he had gently disentangled himself and asked "What do we do now?" He had meant it as a nice way of acknowledging his ardor, while gallantly leaving the choice up to her. But when she replied knowingly, "We discuss our body fluids," all desire drained from him instantly. He took a few unnerved steps around the stranger's cluttered living room, noting an arrangement of peculiar tin toys which she obviously considered evidence of an idiosyncratic eye. They struck him as childish.

"We what?" he had said.

"You read the papers." She rose, and plucked a small biplane from her collection, and twirled the propeller with one finger. He almost expected her to draw blood with the corroded blade and present it for his inspection. "Mine check out," she said, glancing up at him. She smiled. "I'm a responsible person." Her speech seemed cold and scripted. He wanted to bolt, but before he found an exit line she had tucked the toy in his jacket pocket and was kissing him again, slipping her hands under his shirt. "You aren't interested in my antibody status?" she asked.

"No," he said, tangling his fingers in the curly hair around her neck, matted with dance-floor sweat. He kissed her throat. "You're so nice and tall."

"I'm interested in yours."

He disengaged himself, crossed the room, and inspected her bookshelf: a predictable assortment of fashionable titles.

"It's not exactly the Summer of Love, anymore," she had said. And he found himself being catechized and lectured about sero-conversion and population profiles and epidemiology by a woman who had thrown herself at him only moments earlier.

When he recalled the tense sex that they had eventually nego-tiated, he mainly remembered her wounded reaction to his frank report on latex and pleasure. And he saw her crouching over his penis with a revolting air of self-sacrifice, as if she were about to sip poison. He remembered the rational, confident tone in which she had patiently explained the simple solution of voluntary test-ing and full disclosure, and the baleful look on her face when he pointed out that such a scheme presumed monogamy and com-mitment.

Since then he had felt a bit contrite—his behavior, he decided, had been somewhat retrograde. "You shouldn't have complained about the condom," Arliss had informed him. "And you shouldn't have suggested she was working out some other issue through this. Hysterical sexuality. Jesus."

"I never said hysteria."

"Bisexual ambivalence? Adult heterosexuality as contamina-tion? You had your little theory."

But the fact that it was his theory didn't mean it wasn't true. He remembered her Dartmouth boy stories, and her nasty anecdotes about predatory professors and other assorted jerks. He felt like she was dusting off a spot for him in her gallery of pathogenic agents and beasts. Plus she had been impatient. She had treated him like an irresponsible dope. She had acted like a sleek, *au courant* denizen of the fast lane, while he was an out-of-it square, a yahoo, a geezer. Gillian had not thrown up these roadblocks. "I assume you consort with neither drug addicts nor other boys," she had said, working a womanly hand under the waistband of his underwear. "And I have led a blameless life."

Lewis scanned the dimly lit faces of his students, many of whose lives were probably heaped with blame. How did they handle these things? Did they have suave rituals? Code words? Implicit understandings?

"You see," said the theory student. She punched the remote control and froze the picture. "Look at her mouth."

Lewis ended the class with what he thought were lame, canned remarks about the contradictions inherent to radical art in a repressive culture. With a familiar mixture of relief and contempt he watched his students ardently write down some version of his words. A few nodded intensely as they bore down on their felt-tips. They seemed satisfied as they stuffed their notebooks into their bags and shuffled out into the dusk. After they had gone, he read a page of scattered notes that someone had abandoned on the seminar table—a disconnected list of phrases: "Figure of woman/state apparatus," "Politically effective *and* compromised?" and "Radical art + Repression = Contradiction. Adorno?" This didn't mean, Lewis told himself firmly, that nobody had learned anything. He had done a credible job in one of those difficult moments that tested a teacher's mettle. The filmmaker and the theorist had exited together, trying to agree on something, saying, "Exactly," and "That's what's crucial."

It was dark when Lewis passed under Boys and into his building and climbed the several flights to his apartment. When he switched on a lamp and put down his briefcase, he was suffused with a delicious sense of solitude. His rooms were in the high school's old gymnasium—he had high windows, skylights in the distant ceiling, and sprung floors, built to give under the impact of basketball players. A perfect place for a dance party, and he had meant to give one ever since he moved in.

Lewis drew the curtains over all but the skylights and punched on his answering machine. There was a message from a student asking if his letter of recommendation was done. Gillian wanted to know if they could make it eight instead of seven on Friday. She and the sitter had got their wires crossed, but the girl had promised to stay until two. Then Luther's voice: "This is your only son, here to inform you that you can't call an answering machine collect." And Phoebe's resolute voice announced that she had a few follow-up questions to last night's phone call. He could reach her at home all evening; she'd appreciate it. "You owe me this."

Lewis had a can of clams and a box of spaghetti in his cupboard, and a few inches of leftover white wine in the refrigerator—all the ingredients for one of his specialties. He rifled through his box of cassettes for Phoebe's Motown tape, to give it one last listen. As he moved competently around his kitchen, he found himself dancing in spurts to the familiar music. An impossibly young Michael Jackson started to sing and, at a favorite refrain, Lewis put down the bottle of wine and the wooden spoon, and raised his hands, thrusting them lightly into the air, while he bent at the knee.

On their first date, Phoebe had led him to a converted fire station with a kitchen and bar at one end and an all-female rock-and-roll band at the other—the Neo-Boys, it said on their drum, in jagged pink letters. The place was filled with energetic people in their teens, their twenties, and their thirties, and it had pleased and excited him to be there. He had not felt out of place, and that realization had pleased him, too.

They ate Mexican food and talked about movies they'd seen recently. She moaned about procrastinating referee readers for the journal the Media Arts Center put out—she seemed proud to be doing a little editing—and she fumed grandly about lousy academic writers who were overinvested in their own convoluted prose. He inquired about her lingering dissertation, and she said, "My dissertation is a mess," and miserably dragged a tortilla chip across some guacamole.

"Hollywood does Vietnam. Such an interesting topic," he had said, encouragingly. "Are you focusing on any particular movies?"

"I've got sort of a chapter on rock music soundtracks. Some stuff on voice-over narration. The good black soldier who always gets killed. A few pages on helicopters and credit sequences. So far it doesn't add up to squat. I don't have a coherent take on the genre or the period."

"Are you going to write about what they do—or don't do—with the anti-war movement back home?"

"Good question," she said, nodding. She squirmed a bit and sat up straighter. "Did you see *Born on the Fourth of July?*" As she gave him her line on that movie he saw that she had one of those changeable faces that could be opaque as lard or expressive as Garbo. He wanted to ruffle her dark, shiny curls. Touch her chin. Tell her to lighten up. Not be so hard on herself.

He told her how two of the Weatherpeople had spent a few underground days with him and Catherine at their place in Berkeley once. But Luther had been little, and it had seemed risky to put them up for very long.

"Wow," she said, impressed, and asked a lot of questions.

She told him that she lived alone. She had recently broken up with a guy that she had lived with since college. They had tried to put things back together, but they hadn't pulled it off. They were still friends, though.

Lewis described his exemplary divorce and encouraged her to maintain a connection with her old boyfriend, if that was what she wanted to do. It had been difficult for him and Catherine, but they were very glad, after all these years, that they had made the effort. Catherine was his best friend, and he was hers. Phoebe brightened at this. "That's how I want it to be with me and Sam," she said, fiddling with the little plastic bull that dangled from the neck of their bottle of Spanish wine. "You haven't gotten married again?" The bull slipped from its satiny tether and Phoebe brought it to her mouth and bit one white horn.

"No," said Lewis.

"You were married such a long time." She carefully balanced the bull on all fours next to the guacamole. It cast a romantic shadow across the greasy table. "It must be hard." She started looking glum again and he refilled both their glasses. "I can't imagine ever loving anybody the way I love Sam. When I allow myself to think that this is really the end of all that, that I am going to live my life without him, I feel like a boat person. I feel like I've lost my culture and my language. That there was this little village someplace where I grew up, and now it's blown to smithereens and I'm the only person left to remember it. That wherever I go, whatever I do, whoever else I'm with, I'm some kind of refugee." She plucked at her shirt. Hawaiian, splashed with ukuleles and orchids and coconuts. "Does that make any sense? Do you know what I mean?"

"Yes," Lewis had said, thinking it made plenty of sense. "I do."

"You know what it's like when you feel like you grew up with someone? When you learned whole vocabularies with that person? Painting, for instance. I took maybe one art history class in college. Same for him. But painting is something that Sam and I learned to look at together. It's what we would do when we traveled. We read the same books and articles; we went to the same shows. And so there's a whole history of responses there, and when I think of going though my life looking at painting without him, it just seems too unbearably sad." She threw herself back against the high bench, and smiled crookedly. "Am I being too self-absorbed? Depressing?"

"No," Lewis said. "I'm interested." In fact, he had been moved.

"It's a bad attitude to have, I know. I mean if I don't stop mythologizing what we had I'll never move on." She reached out and lightly tapped the hand with which he held his wine glass.

"What went wrong between you two?"

She had looked around the room in an agitated fashion. "Believe me, you don't want to know."

The Neo-Boys were tuning up, checking plugs and mikes and joshing with some fans. "You're still very much in this, aren't you?" Lewis had said to her. "It's going to take you a long time to get out of it. And that's as it should be."

She had seemed alarmed. "It's been a long time already. A friend of mine, someone who cares about us both, said to me last week, 'Face it, honey, it is time to clear out. It's Saigon. 1975. And the helicopters are on the embassy roof.'"

One of the Neo-Boys, dressed in a black tutu, with stiff, sparkling red hair, approached the microphone, and began to sing in a raspy, high-pitched voice. "'Lip-Synch,'" Phoebe said. "One of their hits." And she excused herself for a moment.

The drummer began to whale away, and Lewis wondered if Luther was better. The two guitarists, wearing matching mod, silver-sequined, tunic-and-pants outfits, executed neat dance duets while they thrashed their instruments. "Boat person," Lewis repeated to himself. It wasn't a bad metaphor, really. He had felt that way for three, four years after Catherine had moved out, taking Luther, and his pint-sized clothes, and all his primary-colored clutter. All through his complicated affair with Abby. He remembered the stricken look on her face whenever he whispered "Cath," or when he would lapse into one of his distant, morose moods. It had been a terrible thing for Abby. It had damaged her. It was years—until he moved back east, really—before Catherine really seemed part of his past. Before he began feeling complete.

The floor filled with dancers. As Lewis wondered if he would be able to do anything but make a fool of himself to this music, two drunk, hearty young women, wearing layers of gauzy shifts and bangles, trooped over to his table and asked him to dance. He hesitated for a moment, and then joined them. When Phoebe returned she looked momentarily abandoned, then simply quizzical and amused. She sat down sportingly and reached for her glass, but the two girls drew her onto the floor. "Come *on*," they said, and the four of them danced together for one raucous song. One of the women said, "You guys are great." She put her arm around her friend's shoulders. "She just moved here. From San Diego. This week."

The drunk woman from California said, "Jeez you two are tall. Are you married?"

Lewis and Phoebe looked at each other and laughed. "Only the first time we've gone out," he said to Phoebe.

"Cali*for*nia," Phoebe said, turning to him, rolling her eyes and shimmying her hands helplessly around her ears.

During the last years of the Truman presidency, Lewis had trudged grimly off to a high-school gymnasium every other Friday night to study the waltz, the cha-cha, the jitterbug, and the lindy. He had learned how to ask a girl to dance, how to lead, how to cut in, and the zones of a girl's body where it was permissible to place one's hands. And then, after he was cut loose from all instruction, dancers stopped touching each other. He learned to twist. He held his arms crooked in a jogger's position at his waist, his hands in fists. After the welcome eclipse of the twist, which had been hard on a knee he had wrenched in a Cornell game in fifty-four, dancers started moving their legs any which way. Lewis had reintroduced into his repertoire staccato versions of his old waltz and lindy steps, but he never figured out what to do with his hands. They seemed eternally stranded in that waist-level jogging position where the twist had beached them. For variation, he occasionally raised one arm above his head. Then, in one of those moments of gratuitous marital cruelty for which there is no forgiveness, Catherine had mocked his dancing to friends. They sat in a seafood restaurant next door to a disco in L.A. She said, "Lewis does his own patented dance. It's called 'The A Train.'" Lewis and the friends had looked uncomprehending. "You know," Catherine said, actually rising from her seat at the laden table, dragging in her wake a corner of the tablecloth which clung to her skirt, forcing Lewis to reach out and save the whole meal from being whisked to the floor. She raised one hand as if she were grasping a subway commuter strap, bent her knees and vibrated. "I'm taking the A Train," she sang out. Ever since that night Lewis had kept his hands in his jogging position.

Phoebe was a marvelous dancer. Her long slim arms snaked and syncopated in mysterious choreography. With unabashed admiration Lewis mirrored her movements. She put her hands on his shoulders and drew him close. "You know what's the best advice I ever got about dancing?" she yelled over the music. "A friend told me this. He said, 'You know those gestures the stewardesses make during the safety speech? They point out the emergency exits.'" Phoebe extended her arms in a wide funnel and her hands became blades, slicing towards the far corners of the room. "'They show you where the life preservers are.'" She stretched her arms directly over her head and pointed at the life preservers with pulsing index fingers. "My friend said to me, 'We have to take our culture's eloquent gestures where we find them.'" She dipped, and her hands cut through the air like fins. "He's dead now." She crossed her wrists in front of her face, in what was perhaps a stylized gesture of mourning, embracing the memory of her dead friend.

As his clams sizzled in the wine, and Michael Jackson lamented that it was too late, Lewis dropped his knees, and raised his hands, and sliced the air. Could that possibly be the best advice about dancing anyone would ever give him? He pointed his index fingers at the life preservers. He reached up and jerked down hard on the emergency oxygen supply. He cupped one hand loosely over his mouth and passed the other behind his head, as if adjusting the elastic strap, and he breathed in deeply. He kept dancing like that for a few bars, with his eyes shut, and his arms cradling his skull.

CONDOMS

Ronald Wallace

She says the book she is reading is gross.
She says she won't tell me what "gross" is.
Hours later, at bedtime, she asks about condoms.
I don't tell her
about the first rubber I ever saw,
fished out of a St. Louis drainage ditch in 1956,
dripping with sewage and ooze,
or about how Johnny Ferretti
blew them up like balloons
for the girls at the Country Day grade school,
or how "for the prevention of disease only"
we'd buy them in the men's room
of Bob Winston's Skelley Station
and keep them like IDs in our wallets.
Instead, I slip over them
that slick word, *prophylactics,*
and tell her they are a birth control device
used by two people making love.
When I bend down to kiss her
she pulls her head under the blankets.
Okay, she grimaces. *That's* gross.

Anne Rice

WELL, IT WAS perfectly obvious which marvelous human experience was meant to come now. But I could feel nothing for her. Nothing. I smiled, and I began to take off my clothes. I peeled off the overcoat, and was immediately cold. Why wasn't she cold? I then took off the sweater and was immediately horrified by the smell of my own sweat. *Lord God, was it really like this before?* And this body of mine had looked so clean.

She didn't seem to notice. I was grateful for that. I then removed my shirt and my shoes and my socks and my pants. My feet were still cold. Indeed, I was cold and naked, very naked. I didn't know whether or not I liked this at all. I suddenly saw myself in the mirror over her dressing table, and I realized that this organ was of course utterly drunk and asleep.

Again, she didn't seem surprised.

"Come here," she said. "Sit down."

I obeyed. I was shivering all over. Then I began to cough. The first cough was a spasm, catching me completely by surprise. Then a whole series of coughs followed, uncontrollably, and the last was so violent that it made a circle of pain around my ribs.

"I'm sorry," I said to her.

"I love your French accent," she whispered. She stroked my hair, and let her nails lightly scratch my cheek.

Now, this was a pleasant sensation. I bent my head and kissed her throat. Yes, this was nice also. It was nothing as exciting as

closing on a victim, but it was nice. I tried to remember what it
had been like two hundred years ago when I was the terror of the
village girls. Seems some farmer was always at the castle gates,
cursing me and swinging his fist at me and telling me that if his
daughter was with child by me, I'd have to do something about it!
It had all seemed such wonderful fun at the time. And the girls, oh
the lovely girls.

"What is it?" she asked.

"Nothing," I said. I kissed her throat again. I could smell sweat
on her body too. I didn't like it. But why? These smells were nothing as sharp, any of them, as they were to me in my other body.
But they connected with something in this body—that was the
ugly part. I felt no protection against these smells; they seemed
not artifacts but something which could invade me and contami-
nate me. For instance, the sweat from her neck was now on my
lips. I knew it was, I could taste it and I wanted to be away from
her.

Ah, but this is madness. She was a human being, and I was a
human being. Thank God this would be over Friday. But what
right had I to thank God!

Her little nipples brushed against my chest, very hot and
nubby and the flesh behind them was squashy and tender. I
slipped my arm around her small back.

"You're hot, I think you have a fever," she said in my ear. She
kissed my neck the way I'd been kissing hers.

"No, I'm all right," I said. But I didn't have the slightest idea of
whether or not this was true. This was hard work!

Suddenly her hand touched my organ, startling me, and then
bringing about an immediate sensation. I felt the organ lengthen
and grow hard. The sensation was entirely concentrated, and yet
it galvanized me. When I looked at her breasts now, and down at
the small fur triangle between her legs, my organ grew even more

hard. Yes, I remember this all right; my eyes are connected to it, and nothing else matters now, hmmm, all right. Just get her down on the bed.

"Whoa!" she whispered. "Now that's a piece of equipment!"

"Is it?" I looked down. The monstrous thing had doubled in size. It did seem grossly out of proportion to everything else. "Yes, I suppose it is. Should have known James would have checked it out."

"Who's James?"

"No, doesn't matter," I mumbled. I turned her face towards me and kissed her wet little mouth this time, feeling her teeth through her thin lips. She opened her mouth for my tongue. This was good, even if her mouth was bad tasting. Didn't matter. But then my mind raced ahead to blood. Drink her blood.

Where was the pounding intensity of drawing near the victim, of the moment right before my teeth pierced the skin and the blood spilled all over my tongue?

No, it's not going to be that easy, or that consuming. It's going to go between the legs and more like a shiver, but this is some shiver, I'll say that.

Merely thinking of the blood had heightened the passion, and I shoved her roughly down on the bed. I wanted to finish, nothing else mattered but finishing.

"Wait a minute," she said.

"Wait for what?" I mounted her, and kissed her again, pushing my tongue deeper into her. No blood. Ah, so pale. No blood. My organ slid between her hot thighs, and I almost spurted then. But it wasn't enough.

"I said wait!" she screamed, her cheeks coloring. "You can't do it without a condom."

"What the hell are you saying?" I murmured. I knew the meaning of these words, yet they didn't make much sense. I pushed my hand down, felt the hair opening, and then the juicy wet crack, which seemed deliciously small.

She screamed at me to get off of her, and she shoved at me with the heels of her hands. She looked very flushed and beautiful to me suddenly in her heat and rage, and when she nudged me with her knee, I slammed down against her, then drew up only long enough to ram the organ into her, and feel that sweet hot tight envelope of flesh close around me, making me gasp.

"Don't! Stop it! I said stop it!" she screamed.

But I couldn't wait. What the hell made her think this was the time to discuss such a thing, I wondered, in some vague crazed fashion. Then, in a moment of blinding spasmodic excitement I came. Semen came roaring out of the organ!

One moment it was eternal; the next it was finished, as if it had never begun. I lay exhausted on top of her, drenched with sweat, of course, and faintly annoyed by the stickiness of the whole event, and her panic-stricken screams.

At last I fell over onto my back. My head was aching, and all the evil smells of the room thickened—a soiled smell from the bed itself, with its sagging, lumpy mattress; the nauseating smell of the cats.

She leapt out of the bed. She appeared to have gone mad. She was crying and shivering, and she snatched up a blanket from the chair and covered herself with it and began screaming at me to get out, get out, get out.

"Whatever is the matter with you?" I asked.

She let loose with a volley of modern curses. "You bum, you miserable stupid bum, you idiot, you jerk!" That sort of thing. I could have given her a disease, she said. Indeed she rattled off the names of several; I could have gotten her pregnant. I was a creep, a prick, a putz! I was to clear out of here at once. How dare I do this to her? Get out before she called the police.

A wave of sleepiness passed over me. I tried to focus upon her, in spite of the darkness. Then came a sudden nausea sharper than I'd ever felt. I struggled to keep it under control, and only by a severe act of will managed not to vomit then and there.

Finally, I sat up and then climbed to my feet. I looked down at her as she stood there, crying, and screaming at me, and I saw suddenly that she was wretched, that I had really hurt her, and indeed there was an ugly bruise on her face.

Very slowly it came clear to me what had happened. She had wanted me to use some form of prophylactic, and I'd virtually forced her. No pleasure in it for her, only fear. I saw her again at the moment of my climax, fighting me, and I realized it was utterly inconceivable to her that I could have enjoyed the struggle, enjoyed her rage and her protests, enjoyed conquering her. But in a paltry and common way, I think I had.

The whole thing seemed overwhelmingly dismal. It filled me with despair. The pleasure itself had been nothing! I can't bear this, I thought, not a moment longer. If I could have reached James, I would have offered him another fortune, just to return at once. Reached James . . . I'd forgotten altogether about finding a phone.

"Listen to me, ma chère," I said. "I'm sorry. Things simply went wrong. I know. I'm sorry."

She moved to slap me but I caught her wrist easily and brought her hand down, hurting her a little.

"Get out," she said again. "Get out or I'll call the police."

"I understand what you're saying to me. It's been forever since I did it. I was clumsy. I was bad."

"You're worse than bad!" she said in a deep raw voice.

And this time she did slap me. I wasn't quick enough. I was astonished by the force of the slap, how it stung. I felt of my face where she'd hit me. What an annoying little pain. It was an insulting pain.

"Go!" she screamed again.

I put on my clothes, but it was like lifting sacks of bricks to do it. A dull shame had come over me, a feeling of such awkwardness and discomfort in the slightest gesture I made or smallest word I spoke that I wanted simply to sink into the earth.

Finally, I had everything buttoned and zipped properly, and I had the miserable wet socks on my feet again, and the thin shoes, and I was ready to go.

She sat on the bed crying, her shoulders very thin, with the tender bones in her back poking at her pale flesh, and her hair dripping down in thick wavy clumps over the blanket she held to her breast. How fragile she looked—how sadly unbeautiful and repulsive.

I tried to see her as if I were really Lestat. But I couldn't do it. She appeared a common thing, utterly worthless, not even interesting. I was vaguely horrified. Had it been that way in my boyhood village? I tried to remember those girls, those girls dead and gone for centuries, but I couldn't see their faces. What I remembered was happiness, mischief, a great exuberance that had made me forget for intermittent periods the deprivation and hopelessness of my life.

What did that mean in this moment? How could this whole experience have been so unpleasant, so seemingly pointless? Had I been myself I would have found her fascinating as an insect is fascinating; even her little rooms would have appeared quaint to me, in their worst, most uninspiring details! Ah, the affection I always felt for all sad little mortal habitats. But why was that so!

And she, the poor thing, she would have been beautiful to me simply because she was alive! I could not have been sullied by her had I fed on her for an hour. As it was, I felt filthy for having been with her, and filthy for being cruel to her. I understood her fear of disease! I, too, felt contaminated! But where lay the perspective of truth?

"I am so sorry," I said again. "You must believe me. It wasn't what I wanted. I don't know what I wanted."

"You're crazy," she whispered bitterly without looking up.

"Some night I'll come to you, soon, and I'll bring you a present, something beautiful that you really want. I'll give it to you and perhaps you'll forgive me."

She didn't answer.

"Tell me, what is it you really want? Money doesn't matter. What is it you want that you cannot have?"

She looked up, rather sullenly, her face blotched and red and swollen, and then she wiped at her nose with the back of her hand.

"You know what I wanted," she said in a harsh, disagreeable voice, which was almost sexless it was so low.

"No, I don't. Tell me what."

Her face was so disfigured and her voice so strange that she frightened me. I was still woozy from the wine I'd drunk earlier, yet my mind was unaffected by the intoxication. It seemed a lovely situation. This body drunk, but not me.

"Who are you?" she asked. She looked very hard now, hard and bitter. "You're somebody, aren't you . . . you're not just . . ." But her voice trailed off.

"You wouldn't believe me if I told you."

She turned her head even more sharply to the side, studying me as if it was all going to come to her suddenly. She'd have it figured out. I couldn't imagine what was going on in her mind. I knew only that I felt sorry for her, and I did not like her. I didn't like this dirty messy room with its low plaster ceiling, and the nasty bed, and the ugly tan carpet and the dim light and the cat box reeking in the other room.

"I'll remember you," I said miserably yet tenderly. "I'll surprise you. I'll come back and I'll bring something wonderful for you, something you could never get for yourself. A gift as if from another world. But right now, I have to leave you."

"Yes," she said, "you'd better go."

I turned to do exactly that. I thought of the cold outside, of Mojo waiting in the hallway, and of the town house with its back door shattered off the hinges, and no money and no phone.

JOY

Elizabeth Benedict

In memory: RJH-B

This dear friend who might be positive
though I don't know the etiquette about asking
he mentions over the usual decaf skim cap
at the usual bookstore cafe
that he is editing a book of poems about it.
He says with an ironic smile, a smudge of steamed milk
on his upper lip, "For this I'm going after
the 'A' list of AIDS poets," and we flash
ironic smiles back and forth, like, what a
lousy distinction, like, not exactly
what you hoped would be your highest calling,
your epitaph, but underneath my smile, or behind it,
I'm thinking, and afraid to say, look, I know I'm
not on it, but I, I might have a poem to offer,
though I am a tourist in this country, not a citizen.
You understand the idea just came to me sitting there
in the shadow of the Self-Help Section, with three shelves
on Death and Bereavement, and a revolving rack
of arty greeting cards, evocative pictures for every occasion
including marriage, acute loneliness, and the illness of a pet.
I have not written a poem since college,
it has barely crossed my mind.

Instead I have made up stories hundreds of pages long
that come from people who touched me or left me or
drove me insane with longing or jealousy or sex
or sadness I did not want to shake, grief I wanted
to consume me as if Jonah had chosen the whale.
But I am not allowed to write a novel about you,
another dear friend, we've known each other
since college, the only dorm that wasn't co-ed.
I am under contract not to tell, nearly choking
with your secret, your double life, which is mine now too.
You said once, "I feel like an undercover cop."
You said, "I had dinner with a friend, she was talking
about her divorce, how devastated she is, and then she wanted
to know how I am, and I pretended all I have to worry about
is my mother's Alzheimer's and which Italian tiles
I should choose for my new kitchen floor."
To see us you would think we are only
ordinary girlfriends. Running up phone bills, doing lunch,
giggling, advising, consoling, breathless with talk
like teenagers, though we are middle-aged, women with
serious CVs, mortgages, parents dead and dying,
and two miraculous children between us.

Alone in the car on South Road heading for the lighthouse
for the hell of it, because it's there,
because it's as far as I can drive before the land runs out,
I fixate on joy.
On how if you think about it it's over so fast.
You feel it momentarily, which means "for a moment,"
not "in a moment's time." For about as long as it takes
to watch a wave break or come
or get up and dance when you hear Sam Cooke on the radio

even if you are alone, or take the last wide curve
on this road just before the ocean comes into view
because when it does the water is turquoise
and you think you are hallucinating, you think,
It's not possible that in chilly New England I am allowed
this Technicolor beauty, even momentarily.
It's always a few seconds after that that I wonder
if I would feel it, would care, would know to look
if it had been me instead of you.
The gynecologist who would not touch you.
The dentist who said you ought to be ashamed of yourself.
The man who fled your house as he inclined
his head for a first kiss and you told him.
The blame you heap on yourself because you did not insist
all those years ago when it was only Haitians and gays that
he wear a hat, though you knew there was someone in his past.
The nightly dreams you are drowning, because you told me once
you can go for days without thinking of it
but the terror comes when you sleep.

A poem because
in a rage at me one night when you learned
I had told my husband—my husband for god's sake,
how else could I explain a month of crying
always after sex, how else? —
you said, "You better not put this
in one of your goddamn novels," and I assured you —
I mean I said the words and prayed that I might mean them —
I assured you that I wouldn't.

CONVENIENCES

Ewing Campbell

I POURED A Schweppes into a Styrofoam cup and broke a plastic envelope of concentrate over it. There was plenty of quinine water, but Vernell hadn't reordered the Bitter Lemon. A little swirl of the swizzle stick and I had a bitter lemon tonic to wash down the pain relievers I was about to take. It was just a few steps along the middle aisle to the aspirin and antihistamine section. You get a headache this big and there's nothing you won't try. I had been taking aspirin until my ears were ringing louder than the white noise of the traffic out on McKinney Avenue. I never knew when I got one of these if it was my malaria coming back or allergies. I suffer terrible from allergies, and I picked up malaria when I was stationed in Panama. The army doctor was able to stop it with quinine, but it always came back, and then I'd have to go back on the quinine. It was ruining my ears, but what can you do?

I'd had this throb in my head for most of the week. The bank had called the note they held on my place. You get a little something going for you, like this Quick Stop, and the forces that be can't let you alone. I wasn't getting rich, but I was paying my bills. It's more that a lot can say. I thought there was some mistake, until I went down to see Liedecker at the bank and he just shrugged, throwing his hands up.

What can I say? he said.

I never missed a payment. What's wrong down here anyway? This is America, isn't it?

Sure it is, but times are bad. S&Ls are folding all over the state, and the governor says they could all go under. You put that kind of talk together with a market crash and nobody wants to take a chance.

What are you talking about? I pay my bills. You can look it up.

Look, he said, I did you a favor approving that loan.

Sure you did and I appreciated it.

He was wagging his head and looking down at his desk and his fingernails. I'll be honest with you, Horak. And he leaned across the desk toward me, lowered his voice. Government auditors came in and checked our books and found some loans—like yours—that weren't adequately secured. So they told us to straighten everything out or else. That's why we called your note. It wasn't secured enough.

But you approved it. It must've been adequate.

He shrugged. I was wrong. I was doing a friend a favor. Now we got to undo the favor according to the federal government.

When he saw I was going to protest, he stood up and came around the desk, encouraging me to get up and join him in a walk toward the front door. As he was offering his good-byes, he paused and glanced around before saying in a confidential manner, Horak, we're friends, right?

We're supposed to be friends.

Listen, keep what I'm going to tell you to yourself. If it got back to someone it wasn't supposed to, I could be in a lot of trouble. I'm already in hot water over that loan of yours.

What hot water?

I'm just saying I'm not the most popular loan officer in the bank right now. That could change, but for the moment, I'm not. So just be careful who you say mentioned this.

Mentioned what?

What I'm telling you. He hesitated, then came out with it. Get yourself a lawyer. Vernell's brother is a lawyer, isn't he? You go see him. There's a way out of this, if you get my drift.

Your drift?

Sure, he said, ask Vernell's brother about chapter eleven. He may know something.

That's it? Ask Vernell's lawyer brother about chapter eleven? That's what you're telling me?

He nodded. That's it. You just ask him if there isn't something he can do for you by looking into chapter eleven. With that, he opened the door. Liedecker the gentleman.

That's when the headache started, and it hasn't stopped since. I couldn't get to the aspirin bottle fast enough after that, but it got worse when I told Vernell.

Liedecker's a friend, she said. You talk to Ben. Call him up. He can handle a bankruptcy.

What bankruptcy? I'm not bankrupt.

Where are you going to get the money to pay the bank? You're the one always saying this is America. Well, use the laws. Look at Johns-Manville. Look at Braniff or the Hunt brothers if you need examples. That's what laws are for. To protect business. You let them take your property and you might as well be in Turkey or Iran.

I'm no bankrupt.

Neither is Texaco, but that didn't stop them. Why have a lawyer in the family if you don't use him?

Once Vernell sets her mind, she won't budge. She took the car and went over to see her brother, Ben the lawyer, and left me with the store, which was empty until an old Chrysler pulled up out front and a pudgy man with a red face got out and lugged his case of samples around the front of the car and came in, saying as soon as he entered, Afternoon. I'm Charlie Redd with the Port du Salut Company. He was wearing a pair of plaid pants and a lime green polyester jacket. It looked like one of those blazers the networks make their sportscasters wear on TV.

I looked him over and said, We're not ordering anything.

A big grin broke out on his face. You'd have thought I just told him I'd take everything he could deliver, cash up front.

You do a hell of a business in Diet Coke, don't you? I've been in here when all the secretaries and receptionists and bank tellers and all the stenographers and telephone operators come in from work. You'd think it was a sorority meeting. And everyone of them buying a Diet Coke.

I don't pay much attention, but it's true women like to stop in and get a soft drink on their way home.

Not on their way home, friend. They're all on their way to Shuffles or Friday's or some other watering hole, and they all want to get loosened up. You notice next time. Watch them spill out a third or so of Coke before they get back into their cars.

That's their business.

Sure it is. It's that new open container law making you money. And I'm here to show you how to make more.

We're not taking on any new products. Maybe later, not now.

Don't worry about that, he said. What I want you to see isn't new. It's been around two thousand years. The Romans had it. There're pictures of it on cave walls. The Chinese had it and the Japanese. Fallopius, of the tubes, wrote about it. With that, he hoisted his black case onto the counter and raised the lid, revealing a display shelf of gold and silver foil disks, black packets with a man in evening dress tipping his top hat, and red waxlike disks looking like miniature Gouda samples with black script at an angle saying, *Port du Salut Royal Sheath.*

What is this? I asked. Samples of chocolate? Cheese?

This is your fortune, he said. And he started popping the gold, silver, black, and red wrappers off, leaving a line of rolled condoms on the green baize of the case, the first packaged in powder, the others in some sort of lubricant.

Rubbers? I said. You're selling rubbers?

Safe sex. That's what I'm selling, safe sex. It's what we've come to. It's an idea whose time has come.

French rubbers?

They're American made, with a French name.

Why? Isn't American good enough?

He nodded toward the shelves. What do you see back between the Bran Chex and Wheaties?

I looked at the boxes and saw Fruit & Fibre.

That's it. Roughage is like safe sex. Everyone wants it. So you spell it the French way to make people notice it. The same here. The French and sex go together. So we give our condoms a French moniker. It's good business. We want a sophisticated image.

Jesus, I said. Rubbers. Women don't buy those things. It's only young guys trying to impress their friends with the big lie that they're getting some.

That's where you're wrong. There's fact and there's fiction, and it's my job to put you straight on the facts. The market research is in. Every third buyer's a woman. And that's a fact you can take to the bank.

Not my bank, you can't.

Any bank. We're talking designer fashions. We're talking prestige items and keeping up with the Vanderbilts.

My head was killing me, and the roar in my ears sounded like a field full of grasshoppers. I wondered if I had a fever. Maybe the malaria was coming back after all. You could kill all the parasites in the blood, but you never got the ones in other parts of the body. I'd discovered that all right. I was wishing Vernell was back with the car so I could get out on the freeway. That was the only thing that drowned the din in my ears—the drone of the car engine and the wind and the static on the radio. When I got on the highway, my ears got a break. What I wouldn't have given to see Vernell come in right then.

He pointed at the first one in the line. This is the regular. It'll do in a pinch, but every self-respecting woman will want something more arousing, like the one in the gold foil. That's the special, packed in a spermicidal lubricant for added protection against unwanted pregnancies. It's also got lanolin in the lubricant.

He glanced up at me with that smile of his.

Now this next one is the deluxe, and you can see it's ribbed for greater pleasure. He unrolled the lubricated condom and showed me the ribbed latex. That got me interested. Maybe he had something there after all. What did I know? Maybe it was just the thing a woman wanted.

It's for the sophisticated set, what every man thinks he's supposed to be and every woman wants him to be. My eyes followed his pudgy fingers as they flicked at the black wrapper with the silhouette of the man in evening clothes. I could see the appeal it would have for young urban professionals all right.

This one here. This one is the Royal Sheath, made of lamb's belly. Suggested retail $3.50 each. Protection for real connoisseurs. It'll add sophistication to their lovemaking. Here, look at this. It'll give the right idea.

He pulled out a rolled-up sheet of glossy paper and unfurled a four-color poster of a young woman wearing a man's dress shirt tied up so lots of midriff was showing, tight faded jeans with a suggestive circular impression showing through the denim of her front pocket. In a printed column to the left of her head and face and shoulder were the facts:

PROFESSION: Investment Banker.

PROFILE: Smart, bold, knows what's up, not afraid
   to take risks, but knows when to pay it safe.
MOST RECENT CONVERSATION: The Persian Gulf.
LAST BOOK READ: *Cultural Literacy*, E.D. Hirsch.
HER PREFERRED PROTECTION: Port du Salut. "The
   Royal Sheath has always been first on my list of
   safe, civilized, and sensual necessities."

You see what I mean? This, right away, gives the idea she's culturally literate if she's carrying Port du Salut, ready to discuss foreign affairs and international crises. He passed the poster to me
and held his pudgy hands up toward the display space next to the
cash register, making an image of the poster with his hands. Put
this up right at eye level where every girl that gets a Diet Coke on
her way to wherever will see it and get the message.

You just put the idea in their heads the thing to do is to have
one of these with them at all times. Use your imagination. Can't
you see this looker giving somebody the eye and a smile, asking,
You holding? Meaning, You got a Salut with you? Under the circumstances, who'd be caught without? You'll make a fortune just
off the girls that stop in for a Coke. But it's up to you to make them
see themselves as something they're not. This is the time of the
image. Everything's in the images the magazines package for them.
That or TV. But this is one thing that's more than a fad.

That was easy for him to say. He wouldn't be the one holding
the unsold merchandise if this scare blew over.

I'm not talking scare tactics, he said. This is a prestige issue.
Those girls are going to insist on this item. The next step is personalized packets.

Monogrammed?

The packages. Sure. Take my word for it. Safe sex is as old as
the history books. Besides, sex is too good to mess up. Nobody
wants to lose it. There's a lobby in Kuala Lumpur that puts out

millions every year to keep the latex flowing from Malaysia to Europe and the U.S. It's a billion dollar industry.

Just as I was putting the poster aside, old Mrs. Grosbeck came in and headed straight for the juice shelf without looking at us. You can set your watch by her. Every day like clockwork, in she shuffles at the end of her constitutional, all bent over and bearing down on the five-ounce cans of Sunsweet Prune Juice.

He was still standing there with his hands up showing me where the poster ought to go, and all I could do was watch Mrs. Grosbeck snatch her can of prune juice, turn, and shuffle toward us with her gaze locked on that can like it would get away if she took her eye off it.

Listen, I said, shut that while I ring this up. It won't take a minute.

He nodded knowingly and slammed his case top down so hard it popped back up and scattered four or five silver foil wafers across the counter as Mrs. Grosbeck pushed her can and a dollar at me. She stared at the foil packages. Her attention was fierce, but it could only handle one thing at a time.

What are these? she said and snatched one of them up and stared at it.

My eyes went from her to the sample and over to him. He just shrugged and rolled his eyes.

Samples, I said.

Mints? she asked.

No, I said, samples.

She glared at me. Of what?

I held my hand out, but she clutched the sample to her and shoved the dollar forward. So I took it and rang up the sale, making change.

She scooped up her can and said, I always try free samples. If I like it, I'll let you know.

She pulled back and started for the door, but nobody said anything until she reached it.

Look, lady, he said.

Mrs. Grosbeck, I said, wait. Can we talk? But she was out the door and gone.

My muscles had started aching somewhere between the poster and Mrs. Grosbeck. And now I could feel the sweat popping out on my face. It wasn't the first time the thought occurred to me, but suddenly everything began to look like another relapse. A chill hit me. Then I began to shake. I saw his eyes get big and that smile slide off his round red face.

Say, is something bothering you? he said.

My ears. I don't know what's wrong with them. They won't stop roaring.

He stared at me a second and said, What it is is tinnitus. That's what's wrong with them, tinnitus. Isn't there something you can take?

I shook my head and tried to stop trembling.

This isn't the first time, is it?

It happens some, now and then.

What do you do when it gets like this?

The only thing that helps is to drown it out.

How do you do that?

I drive. He looked astounded. I get in the car and drive around, letting the noise of the wind and traffic drown out the ringing. But I can't this time cause Vernell took the car over to her brother's.

What about a taxi? You could call a cab, couldn't you?

That was an idea. It never occurred to me before, but it might work in an emergency. I was thinking it over, staring past him at nothing, when his old Chrysler caught my eye. There was a car made for racket. The seals around the doors would be shot. The motor would be full of knocks, the body full of rattles. If it had a radio, you could bet your last dollar it was going to have static in it when you turned it on.

I looked at him, then back at his old heap. I looked long and hard at that old car and then back at him.

Say, I said.

He must have seen what I was thinking because his head was already wagging back and forth. I have these to sell or else, he said.

Maybe I could take on a new line of products after all, I said.

I don't think I could do anything like that, he said.

A new line might be just the thing. If you saw your way clear to . . . maybe I could.

You could?

I'm pretty sure I could.

He looked down at the rubbers he had opened and the poster that I had put aside. I don't know.

You want to sell them, don't you?

Oh yes, but I don't know about driving around town. I don't have much gas. How long would you want to ride for?

I could get you some gas.

And you think you could take the whole line?

I'd want to take on the whole line. Sure. If I was going to carry them, I'd want the whole line.

Well, maybe I could. Wait a second, let me think. His look went off into space, then came back to me and he said, Sure. Why not? But what about your store? You're not going to just leave it unattended, are you?

We'll close. Lock it up. You get like this, nothing else matters. Just leave your sample case there and we'll get it later. All right?

I guess so if that's what you want.

It'll be okay here. What'd you say your name was?

Redd. Charlie Redd.

Well, come on, Charlie, I said. You drive. I'll ride. I ushered him out and locked the door, not waiting for him to get into his car first. There wasn't much use standing on ceremony now, not with the pounding in my head and aching in my body. I wanted to get under way as fast as he could get it going.

Your radio works, doesn't it? I asked.

Not very good, he said.

Good, I said. Turn it on.

He reached over and hit one of the buttons and a country and western song came on, crackling with static. Then the ignition kicked in and we were on our way.

Go out Stemmons north, I said. We can hit 635 and head east. Just get it up to cruising speed so I can relax.

We headed for the freeway. The shakes were still with me and getting worse. And so was the aching. There was a time in Panama when the fever would get so bad it paralyzed me. I couldn't do anything but stay in my hammock with an ice bag on my neck and one vodka tonic after another till I fell asleep with the racket of birds screeching in the treetops of the jungle.

I'd wake before dawn and it would be quiet and I'd be exhausted, but the fever would have broken some time in the night. I'd just lie there, wrung out, thirsty, my mouth tasting like bile. That was the old days, before I met Vernell.

He glanced over at me, but I kept my eyes on the road, trying to hold myself in.

Are you all right? he asked. You're not going to die on me, are you?

Not as long as you're driving, I won't.

Just as we lumbered up the ramp and onto the expressway, there was a screech of brakes right on top of us. A new Lincoln swerved around us, the driver leaning on the horn with one hand, shooting us the finger with the other.

My stomach started to cramp, but I held tight, as tight as I could. He was a nervous wreck by now. Don't stop, I said. Just keep driving.

Panama. You could stand on the beach, looking out across the Pacific and watch the sun seem to rise in the west because the coastline doubled back on itself. That was Panama. Everything upside down, backward—the sun rising in the west, ships sailing uphill, lock by lock. I thought of all that latex flowing through the Canal, coming from Malaysia, each lock lifting the load, bringing it up, and I said, If it'll make you feel any better, you can give me the history of rubbers while you drive. Just don't stop.

I barely got this out because my teeth were chattering. Then I shut up and listened for the roaring in my ears. But it was gone. And for the first time in a week, I put the store and the bank and Vernell's brother, the lawyer, out of my mind and just listened to the wind blowing through that old wreck of a Chrysler and the sweet sounds of clanging and banging as the traffic surrounded us.

It was a convenient treatment for something I knew I was going to have to live with the rest of my life. The medics had told me the quinine could get it out of the blood where it caused all the trouble and aspirin would help with the fever and pain, but both the quinine and the aspirin would ruin my ears. It was a trade-off I'd have to live with, they said, because you could never get it completely out of the body. That's what I was remembering when suddenly I thought of the lubricated condom with the raised wales he had held up. I don't know why, but I did. And right then I decided I'd try it out with Vernell and see if there was anything to it. Maybe there was. Who knows? Maybe those ridges were everything he said they were. If aspirin could make my ears ring and certain little parasites in my blood could give me a fever, maybe a few ribs and grooves could put a little magic back in our lives.

I thought about that and caught myself smiling. For a moment I had forgotten all about the shakes and the cramps and was looking forward to seeing Vernell. For a moment I didn't have a trouble in the world.

SINCE '81

Alison Stone

We dress for sex in rubber—
Condoms, gloves and dental dams.
We kiss without sharing,
Other lips something to push off from
As we swim solitary laps.

We merge without touching
Safe in plastic
Eyes closed, dreaming
Of something tender, scary
As a memory of birth.

Afterwards
Your gloved hand
Strokes my hair.
The strands catch,
Pull out
And my eyes spill tears
Which may or may not be safe.

DEVICES

James Seay

The one of lambskin
I left in Sardis Lake that night:
tell the girl whose body print surrounds it
I said
come back to the water.

Whatever came between us . . .
nothing's been settled.

I don't understand
what passes between women and me
any more than I used to.
Naked and proud, I'm still the sailor
who had his body
tattooed like an admiral's uniform.

One woman told me a little pain
never hurt anybody.
Well, it doesn't go very far either.
The sharpest tooth I ever felt
left only a bruise
easing along under the thumbnail
like an old turtle,
purple and dry
and almost a friend by the end.

EXCERPTS FROM
PRAISE

Andrew McGahan

LATER WE WENT out onto the verandah. Dave got us all beers. I was dizzy and nauseous again, but it was better than the first time.

We sat there for an hour or so, mostly quiet.

Cynthia was holding my hand, playing with my hair. 'Well,' she said, 'What'll we do? Another bath?'

'I guess so . . . we could try the tub at my place. It's not as big, but it'd be something different at least.'

'Okay.'

We got in the Kingswood. Cynthia was driving. The roads were quiet. Sunday afternoon.

'We should get some lubricant,' she said. 'My cunt hurts enough as it is.'

'Where do you get lubricant from?'

She looked at me. Shook her head. 'You get it from a chemist.'

We found a chemist. I went in. Cynthia didn't want to deal with the counter staff. She was embarrassed about her skin. Her face. It was bad, all that contact the night before. Sex was lethal to her.

The brand she wanted was called K-Y Personal Lubricant. I went in and wandered around the shelves. I was feeling good. I looked at all the colours, all the boxes. I moved smoothly down the aisles. It was all going well. Eventually I found the stuff amongst the tampons and pads. It came in a blue and white tube, in a blue and white box. I took one up to the counter. The woman looked at me.

I said, 'I'll just take this, thanks.'

I flicked up my hand to show her the box. I was moving faster than I realised. The tube flew out, up into the air. I watched it spin there. It floated. The woman reached out and caught it.

We looked at each other.

'Fine,' she said.

I paid up. I saw that the shelves behind the counter were lined with boxes of condoms. Cynthia and I were not using condoms. She was on the pill. She admitted she wasn't all that regular with the doses. I thought, because of that, condoms might've been a practical idea. But Cynthia said she hated them, and practicality was such an odious thing to labour under . . .

I got back to the car and gave her the K-Y.

'They've got a million condoms in there,' I said. 'You sure I shouldn't get some?'

'No! You just can't do it with those things. I'm not going to get pregnant anyway. I've been fucking for years without condoms. I'm infertile, I must be. All those drugs I've been on, the cortisone and the smack and the speed . . . they've ruined me.'

'Okay.'

'God, what am I saying. I'm never going to have children. Fucking is all I've got left.'

'You've got much more than that, Cynthia.'

As for diseases, it was a bit late to be worrying. Anything one of us had, the other had it by now. . . .

• •

For a while, things weren't too bad.

If I was trapped with Cynthia, there was no need for it to be all pain. Just as long as I didn't struggle. She was good company. We got on well. It was only when I was very drunk, or sometimes when we fucked, that I understood how depressed I was.

I needed to be alone for a time.

It wasn't going to happen.

Cynthia's next period arrived. Her periods had been irregular ever since the abortion, but this time it was bad. Painful. The premenstrual cramps went on for days. And when the bleeding came it was black, clotted and dead. It was wrong. She was worried. I was worried. I kept my mouth away from it.

By that time I knew Cynthia's cunt almost as well as I knew my own prick. In fact, I knew it better. I'd never seen my penis from all the angles. That honour was Cynthia's. She had even discovered a mole on the underside of my balls. I'd never known it was there. It was *her* mole. Maybe it was all hers. Balls, prick, the lot of it.

In which case, her cunt was mine. The whole thing, right down to its dark and dangerous depths. I had four months of exploration behind me. I'd stretched and pulled and poked. I knew my way around. I knew how deep it was, how wide it could go, how far I could suck the lips back into my mouth before it really started to hurt.

Cynthia's cunt was my responsibility. I could tell when something was wrong with it. And something was definitely wrong with it.

It was my tongue that picked it up. It was two or three nights after the bleeding had stopped. We were fucking in the dark. I was down between her legs. My mouth was latched on. And my tongue encountered lumps. Dozens of them. The inside of her vagina felt like the sole of a sandshoe.

I waited until after we'd finished. Then I told her about it.

'Lumps?'

'Lumps.'

She sat up and switched on the light, then turned her back to me and examined herself. 'Oh. Oh yuck.'

'What?'

'Look at this.'

She turned around and I got down between her legs. She spread the lips. I looked in. The skin was spotted with what looked like pimples. Small, white-headed pimples.

'Jesus,' I said.

'How far back do they go?'

'Far as I can see.'

She took her fingers away and lay back. 'What's *wrong* with me?'

I didn't know.

I drove her up to Family Planning the next day. We went to Family Planning for everything like this. They were free. Cynthia wasn't looking forward to it.

'I *hate* vaginal examinations.'

'The doctor won't enjoy it either.'

'How would you know?'

'I know. It's all the doctors in the family. Between them they've gone through hundreds of vaginas. When they were interns it got so bad that they'd run screaming from any woman with vaginal problems. There's a lot that can go wrong with vaginas. They bleed, they stink, they exude pus, they collapse, they grow tumours, they fall *out*.'

'Thanks. Thanks a lot. It's what I need to know. It's okay for men. Men have it all hanging out, ready to look at.'

Which was true. There was only one risk with having exterior sexual organs—they could be chopped off, or crushed, or mangled. The family doctors had a lot of horror stories there, too.

We reached Family Planning and I dropped Cynthia off at the door. I parked and waited. She came walking back along the footpath about half an hour later. She looked upset. She was holding some leaflets. When medical clinics or Social Security gave you leaflets, it was a bad sign.

I opened the door. 'What'd they say?'

'They think I've got genital warts.'

I started the car.

Cynthia lit up. 'I'm sick of this body. Pregnant. Diseased. Why the fuck do I bother?'

'What happens now?'

'They'll burn the warts out.'

'Burn them?'

'With acid.'

'Christ.'

'It's painless. I'm not worried about that. I'm worried about cancer. Warts can cause cervical cancer. They took some tests. I have to go back in a week.'

'Is it likely?'

'They took one look at my sexual history and freaked.'

'Well . . . '

'When I told them about that last period they *really* freaked.'

'Yes, but . . . '

'And when I told them I smoked, and took the pill, and spent half my life on cortisone, they fucking screamed at me.'

'Cynthia . . . '

'I'm gonna die.'

'But what about me?'

'You'll have to get tested too, I suppose.'

'What can happen to a man with genital warts?'

'Cancer of the penis.'

'Oh my *God*.'

'It's a slim chance, I'll admit.'

We drove in silence.

She said, 'I don't think you should get yourself tested.'

'Why not? Cancer of the penis, Cynthia . . . '

'They'll just tell you to start fucking with condoms. If I'm going to die I'm not gonna have my last few fucks with condoms. Wait till I'm gone. Wait till I'm dead.'

'What if you don't die?'

'Then wait till I *leave*. I refuse to fuck rubber!' . . .

• •

Next day it was time to face some realities. I went down to the STD clinic. It was in an old building on the quieter end of Adelaide Street in the City. The sign outside said Special Clinic. I went inside, walked up the stairs and gave my name at the desk. Then I sat down to wait.

There were three other men there. My fellow diseased. My fellow *male* diseased. The women's waiting room was somewhere else. It made sense. The sexes were embattled enough as it was.

I read some leaflets, some magazines. I thought about the warts. There were no growths on my penis, but I was sure to have the virus. It was my first sexual disease. If that wasn't a sign of manhood, what was? I should've felt *good*. The waiting room was an initiation chamber for *men*.

I didn't feel good. I was sad. I felt like a fool. They called my name and I got up and followed the doctor in.

My doctor was a woman. She sat me down and asked me what the problem was. I told her about Cynthia and the warts.

'Okay,' she said, pulling out a form, 'I'll just get some details.'

'Fine.'

'How many sexual partners have you had over the last twelve months?'

'Three.'

'Use condoms?'

'No. Not with Cynthia.'

'Uh-huh. Ever used intravenous drugs?'

'A couple of times. Not lately.'

'Did you share syringes?'

'No'

'Any homosexual experiences?'

'Barely. Just the once.'

'Any anal intercourse?'

'No.'

'Any anal intercourse with your female partners?'

'Yes.'

'Any idea about their sexual history?'

'In some cases, prolific.'

'Had any sexually transmitted diseases in the past?'

'No.'

'Any current symptoms that you might think are due to a sexual disease?'

'No.'

'Do you want an AIDS test?'

'Should I?'

'You could be at risk. It couldn't hurt.'

'Okay.'

And there it was. My life.

'Okay. Take off your pants and lie on the table.'

The doctor turned away to a table of instruments. I pulled down my jeans. There it was, the organ in question, my penis. Retracted and wrinkled and tiny and pink. I tweaked it a couple of times. It didn't relax. It knew what was coming.

I lay down.

She came over, pulling on a pair of thin plastic gloves. She took my prick in one hand, bent down over me and scrutinised it. The gloves felt cool. I put my arms behind my head, stared at the ceiling.

She was twisting it around, looking from all the angles. Then she started on my balls, rolling them, squeezing them, lifting the sac. 'Have you always had this mole?'

'Apparently.'

'Has it changed shape lately?'

'Well, I don't really see it that much.'

'You should keep an eye on it. Use a mirror.'

She stood up. 'I can't see any warts. What I'll do now is douse your penis with vinegar and then look at it under a UV light. That should show up any warts that are too small for me to see. They're like that sometimes.'

She went over to the table and came back with some strips of tissue soaked in vinegar. 'This'll feel cold,' she said. She wrapped them round. She was right about the cold.

'I'll have to leave it like that for a while.'

We waited.

'So what do you do with yourself, Gordon?'

'Nothing. I'm unemployed.'

Silence.

I said, 'This must be thrilling for you, day after day.'

'Well, at least I'm on men today. Men are a lot easier.'

'That makes sense. Does it get busy?'

'Sometimes. Not today. Mondays and Fridays are the big days. Friday everyone comes in to make sure they're okay for the weekend, then Monday they all come in again to make sure they're okay *after* the weekend. They don't have a clue.'

We waited again.

Then she took the wrapping off. She pulled the lamp down over my hips and switched it on. The plastic fingers took me again. Probed, pulled.

'Ah-ha.'

I looked down. 'What?'

'Here's a little one. See?'

I looked. My penis had grown a bit. She was pointing to an area about halfway down the shaft.

'I can't see anything.'

She peered at it again. 'It is only a small one.'

'What now?'

'We'll get rid of it. I'll dab it with some acid. It'll turn black after a couple of days, then drop off.'

'Drop off?'

'It won't *hurt*.'

She went off, came back with a small bottle and a cotton bud. She dabbed the wart with a clear cold liquid. It didn't sizzle, it didn't burn.

'Now,' she said, 'this one will fall off, but you'll have to come back regularly for check-ups. You'll be infectious for about a year, so if you do have sex with anyone, you *must* use condoms.'

'I don't think it's likely to happen.'

'Even so, don't forget.'

'I won't.'

'Okay. Now we'll test for all the other diseases. Syphilis, gon-orrhoea, herpes, a few more of the regular ones. Okay?'

'Okay.'

She went back to the table, picked up a scalpel and a small, sharp hook.

She held them up. She looked at me.

'This might hurt a little.'

'Hey. No one told me there'd be *hooks*.'

'Ah. Well, there has to be *some* pain for the men. We have to be fair, don't you think?'

She pried open the eye of my penis, and sank the hook in.

After she was finished I went back into the waiting room to wait for the results. My prick was stinging. Cynthia's revenge. The doctor hadn't even noticed the tattoo, right on the head: 'Property of Cynthia Lamonde. NO TRESPASSING.'

It was an unworthy thought. I deserved more than a stinging penis. A stinging penis was something to be amused by. I thought about Cynthia's cramps after the abortion, about the black clotted blood. There was nothing funny there. I read some more magazines. After about twenty minutes the doctor called me back in.

'All clear,' she said. 'Nothing but the warts.'

'Good.'

'Of course the AIDS results will be a couple of weeks yet. You have to come back then for your first check-up anyway.'

'Fine.'

I went back into the street.

ROBERTA SAYS
THE WORLD HAS GONE TO PLASTIC

Martha Elizabeth

These days you might as well be shrink-wrapped at birth.
Everything's sealed for your protection,
aspirin, yogurt, cigarettes.
Nurses wear gloves to draw blood,
dentists won't touch your spit.
Pretty soon people won't even kiss.
The women's group talked about how to be safe
now that bad blood doesn't mean a mean streak anymore.
Someone said, Let's take turns
sheathing a cucumber.
I heard that a man volunteered.
He'd stay erect as long as it took,
calm as a statue, till every woman learned the knack.
He lifted his head like a hero
thinking of it, how they would tremble at first,
become unashamed. He would feel
the difference in their hands. As he dressed,
praised the cookies someone made,
he'd wave off their thanks.
Afterwards, from a distance
they'd nod or wink.
They'd introduce their men to him.
He'd dance at their weddings, swing their children,
take leftovers home from Thanksgiving. Of course

they said no. One of those women
knows all about playing it safe.
She flies solo in a locked house
on the washing machine
as it spins an unbalanced load—
bumping along with whoever comes to mind.

WE DIDN'T

Stuart Dybek

> *We did it in front of the mirror*
> *And in the light. We did it in darkness,*
> *In water, and in the high grass.*
> —"We Did It," YEHUDA AMICHAI

WE DIDN'T IN the light; we didn't in darkness. We didn't in the fresh cut summer grass or in the mounds of autumn leaves or on the snow where moonlight threw down our shadows. We didn't in your room on the canopy bed you slept in, the bed you'd slept in as a child, or in the backseat of my father's rusted Rambler which smelled of the smoked chubs and kielbasa that he delivered on weekends from my Uncle Vincent's meat market. We didn't in your mother's Buick Eight where a rosary twined the rearview mirror like a beaded, black snake with silver, cruciform fangs.

At the dead end of our lovers' lane—a side street of abandoned factories—where I perfected the pinch that springs open a bra; behind the lilac bushes in Marquette Park where you first touched me through my jeans and your nipples, swollen against transparent cotton, seemed the shade of lilacs; in the balcony of the now-defunct Clark Theater where I wiped popcorn salt from my palms and slid them up your thighs and you whispered, "I feel like Doris Day is watching us," we didn't.

How adept we were at fumbling, how perfectly mistimed our timing, how utterly we confused energy with ecstasy.

Remember that night becalmed by heat, and the two of us, fused by sweat, trembling as if a wind from outer space that only we could feel was gusting across Oak Street Beach? Wound in your faded Navajo blanket, we lay soul-kissing until you wept with wanting.

We'd been kissing all day—all summer—kisses tasting of different shades of lip gloss and too many Cokes. The lake had turned hot pink, rose rapture, pearl amethyst with dusk, then washed in night black with a ruff of silver foam. Beyond a momentary horizon, silent bolts of heat lightning throbbed, perhaps setting barns on fire somewhere in Indiana. The beach that had been so crowded was deserted as if there was a curfew. Only the bodies of lovers remained behind, visible in lightning flashes, scattered like the fallen on a battlefield, a few of them moaning, waiting for the gulls to pick them clean.

On my fingers your slick scent mixed with the coconut musk of the suntan lotion we'd repeatedly smeared over one another's bodies. When your bikini top fell away, my hands caught your breasts, memorizing their delicate weight, my palms cupped as if bringing water to parched lips.

Along the Gold Coast, high rises began to glow, window added to window, against the dark. In every lighted bedroom, couples home from work were stripping off their business suits, falling to the bed, and doing it. They did it before mirrors and pressed against the glass in streaming shower stalls, they did it against walls and on the furniture in ways that required previously unimagined gymnastics which they invented on the spot. They did it in honor of man and woman, in honor of beast, in honor of God. They did it because they'd been released, because they were home free, alive, and private, because they couldn't wait any longer, couldn't wait for the appointed hour, for the right time or temperature, couldn't wait for the future, for Messiahs, for peace on earth and justice for all. They did it because of the Bomb, because of pollution, because of the Four Horsemen of the Apocalypse, because extinction might be just a blink away. They did it because it was Friday night. It was Friday night and somewhere delirious music was playing—flutter-tongued flutes, muted trumpets meowing like cats in heat, feverish plucking and twanging, tom-toms, congas, and gongs all pounding the same pulsebeat.

I stripped your bikini bottom down the skinny rails of your legs and you tugged my swimsuit past my tan. Swimsuits at our ankles, we kicked like swimmers to free our legs, almost expecting a tide to wash over us the way the tide rushes in on Burt Lancaster and Deborah Kerr in their famous love scene on the beach in *From Here to Eternity*—a scene so famous that although neither of us had seen the movie our bodies assumed the exact position of movie stars on the sand and you whispered to me softly, "I'm afraid of getting pregnant," and I whispered back, "Don't worry, I have protection," then, still kissing you, felt for my discarded cutoffs and the wallet in which for the last several months I had carried a Trojan as if it was a talisman. Still kissing, I tore its flattened, dried-out wrapper and it sprang through my fingers like a spring from a clock and dropped to the sand between our legs. My hands were shaking. In a panic, I groped for it, found it, tried to dust it off, tried, as Burt Lancaster never had to, to slip it on without breaking the mood, felt the grains of sand inside it, a throb of lightning, and the Great Lake behind us became, for all practical purposes, the Pacific and your skin tasted of salt and to the insistent question that my hips were asking, your body answered yes, your thighs opened like wings from my waist as we surfaced panting from a kiss that left you pleading *oh Christ yes*, a yes gasped sharply as a cry of pain so that for a moment I thought that we *were* already doing it and that somehow I had missed the instant when I entered you, entered you in the bloodless way in which a young man discards his own virginity, entered you as if passing through a gateway into the rest of my life, into a life as I wanted it to be lived *yes* but O then I realized that we were still floundering unconnected in the slick between us and there was sand in the Trojan as we slammed together still feeling for that perfect fit, still in the *Here* groping for an *Eternity* that was only a fine adjustment away, just a millimeter to the left or a fraction of an inch further south though with all the adjusting the sandy Trojan was slipping off and then it was gone but yes you kept repeating although your head was shaking no-not-quite-almost and our hearts were going like mad and you said yes Yes wait . . . Stop!

"What?" I asked, still futilely thrusting as if I hadn't quite heard you.

"Oh, God!" you gasped, pushing yourself up. "What's coming?"

"Julie, what's the matter?" I asked, confused, and then the beam of a spotlight swept over us and I glanced into its blinding eye.

All around us lights were coming, speeding across the sand. Blinking blindness away, I rolled from your body to my knees, feeling utterly defenseless in the way that only nakedness can leave one feeling. Headlights bounded towards us, spotlights crisscrossing, blue dome lights revolving as squad cars converged. I could see other lovers, caught in the beams, fleeing bare-assed through the litter of garbage that daytime hordes had left behind and that night had deceptively concealed. You were crying, clutching the Navajo blanket to your breasts with one hand and clawing for your bikini with the other, and I was trying to calm your terror with reassuring phrases such as, "Holy shit! I don't fucking believe this!"

Swerving and fishtailing in the sand, police calls pouring from their radios, the squad cars were on us, and then they were by us while we sat struggling on our clothes.

They braked at the water's edge, and cops slammed out brandishing huge flashlights, their beams deflecting over the dark water. Beyond the darting of those beams, the far-off throbs of lightning seemed faint by comparison.

"Over there, goddamn it!" one of them hollered, and two cops sloshed out into the shallow water without even pausing to kick off their shoes, huffing aloud for breath, their leather cartridge belts creaking against their bellies.

"Grab the sonofabitch! It ain't gonna bite!" one of them yelled, then they came sloshing back to shore with a body slung between them.

It was a woman—young, naked, her body limp and bluish beneath the play of flashlight beams. They set her on the sand just past the ring of drying, washed-up alewives. Her face was almost totally concealed by her hair. Her hair was brown and tangled in a way that even wind or sleep can't tangle hair, tangled as if it had absorbed the ripples of water—thick strands, slimy-looking like dead seaweed.

"She's been in there a while, that's for sure," a cop with a beer belly said to a younger, crew-cut cop who had knelt beside the body and removed his hat as if he might be considering the kiss of life.

The crew-cut officer brushed the hair away from her face and the flashlight beams settled there. Her eyes were closed. A bruise or a birthmark stained the side of one eye. Her features appeared swollen—her lower lip protruding as if she was pouting.

An ambulance siren echoed across the sand, its revolving red light rapidly approaching.

"Might as well take their sweet-ass time," the beer-bellied cop said.

We had joined the circle of police surrounding the drowned woman almost without realizing that we had. You were back in your bikini, robed in the Navajo blanket, and I had slipped on my cutoffs, my underwear still dangling out of a back pocket.

Their flashlight beams explored her body causing its whiteness to gleam. Her breasts were floppy; her nipples looked shriveled. Her belly appeared inflated by gallons of water. For a moment, a beam focused on her mound of pubic hair which was overlapped by the swell of her belly, and then moved almost shyly away down her legs, and the cops all glanced at us—at you, especially—above their lights, and you hugged your blanket closer as if they might confiscate it as evidence or to use as a shroud.

When the ambulance pulled up, one of the black attendants immediately put a stethoscope to the drowned woman's swollen belly and announced, "Drowned the baby, too."

Without saying anything, we turned from the group, as unconsciously as we'd joined them, and walked off across the sand, stopping only long enough at the spot where we had lain together like lovers, in order to stuff the rest of our gear into a beach bag, to gather our shoes, and for me to find my wallet and kick sand over the forlorn, deflated-looking Trojan that you pretended not to notice. I was grateful for that.

Behind us, the police were snapping photos, flashbulbs throbbing like lightning flashes, and the lightning itself still distant but moving in closer, rumbling audibly now, driving a lake wind before it so that gusts of sand tingled against the metal sides of the ambulance.

Squinting, we walked towards the lighted windows of the Gold Coast, while the shadows of gapers attracted by the whirling emergency lights hurried past up toward the shore.

"What happened? What's going on?" they asked us as they passed without waiting for an answer, and we didn't offer one, just continued walking silently in the dark.

It was only later that we talked about it, and once we began talking about the drowned woman it seemed we couldn't stop.

"She was pregnant," you said, "I mean I don't want to sound morbid, but I can't help thinking how the whole time we were, we almost—you know—there was this poor, dead woman and her unborn child washing in and out behind us."

"It's not like we could have done anything for her even if we had known she was there."

"But what if we *had* found her? What if after we had—you know," you said, your eyes glancing away from mine and your voice tailing into a whisper, "what if after we did it, we went for a night swim and found her in the water?"

"But, Jules, we didn't," I tried to reason, though it was no more a matter of reason than anything else between us had ever been.

It began to seem as if each time we went somewhere to make out—on the back porch of your half-deaf, whiskery Italian grandmother who sat in the front of the apartment cackling before "I Love Lucy" reruns; or in your girlfriend Ginny's basement rec room when her parents were away on bowling league nights and Ginny was upstairs with her current crush, Brad; or way off in the burbs, at the Giant Twin Drive-In during the weekend they called Elvis Fest—the drowned woman was with us.

We would kiss, your mouth would open, and when your tongue flicked repeatedly after mine, I would unbutton the first button of your blouse revealing the beauty spot at the base of your throat which matched a smaller spot I loved above a corner of your lips, and then the second button that opened on a delicate gold cross—that I had always tried to regard as merely a fashion statement—dangling above the cleft of your breasts. The third button exposed the lacy swell of your bra, and I would slide my hand over the patterned mesh, feeling for the firmness of your nipple rising to my fingertip, but you would pull slightly away, and behind your rapid breath your kiss would grow distant, and I would kiss harder trying to lure you back from wherever you had gone, and finally, holding you as if only consoling a friend, I'd ask, "What are you thinking?" although, of course, I knew.

"I don't want to think about her but I can't help it. I mean it seems like some kind of weird omen or something, you know?"

"No, I don't know," I said. "It was just a coincidence."

"Maybe if she'd been further away down the beach, but she was so close to us. A good wave could have washed her up right beside us."

"Great, then we could have had a *menage à trois*."

"Gross! I don't believe you just said that! Just because you said it in French doesn't make it less disgusting."

"You're driving me to it. Come on, Jules, I'm sorry," I said, "I was just making a dumb joke to get a little different perspective on things."

"What's so goddamn funny about a woman who drowned herself and her baby?"

"We don't even know for sure she did."

"Yeah, right, it was just an accident. Like she just happened to be going for a walk pregnant and naked, and she fell in."

"She could have been on a sailboat or something. Accidents happen; so do murders."

"Oh, like murder makes it less horrible? Don't think that hasn't occurred to me. Maybe the bastard who knocked her up killed her, huh?"

"How should I know? You're the one who says you don't want to talk about it and then gets obsessed with all kinds of theories and scenarios. Why are we arguing about a woman we don't even know, who doesn't have the slightest thing to do with us?"

"I *do* know about her," you said. "I dream about her."

"You dream about her?" I repeated, surprised. "Dreams you remember?"

"Sometimes they wake me up. Like I dreamed I was at my

nonna's cottage in Michigan. Off her beach they've got a raft for swimming and in my dream I'm swimming out to it, but it keeps drifting further away until it's way out on the water and I'm so tired that if I don't get to it I'm going to drown. Then, I notice there's a naked person sunning on it and I start yelling, 'Help!' and she looks up, brushes her hair out of her face, and offers me a hand, but I'm too afraid to take it even though I'm drowning because it's her."

"God! Jules, that's creepy."

"I dreamed you and I were at the beach and you bring us a couple hot dogs but forget the mustard, so you have to go all the way back to the stand for it."

"Hot dogs, no mustard—a little too Freudian, isn't it?"

"Honest to God, I dreamed it. You go off for mustard and I'm wondering why you're gone so long, then a woman screams a kid has drowned and immediately the entire crowd stampedes for the water and sweeps me along with it. It's like the one time when I was little and got lost at the beach, wandering in a panic through this forest of hairy legs and pouchy crotches, crying for my mother. Anyway, I'm carried into the water by the mob and forced under, and I think, this is it, I'm going to drown, but I'm able to hold my breath longer than could ever be possible. It feels like a flying dream—flying underwater—and then I see this baby down there flying, too, and realize it's the kid everyone thinks has drowned, but he's no more drowned than I am. He looks like Cupid or one of those baby angels that cluster around the face of God."

"Pretty weird. What do you think it means? Something to do with drowning maybe, or panic?"

"It means the baby who drowned inside her that night was a love child—a boy—and his soul was released there to wander through the water."

"You really believe that?"

We argued about the interpretation of dreams, about whether dreams were symbolic or psychic, prophetic or just plain non-sense until you said, "Look, you can believe what you want about your dreams, but keep your nose out of mine, okay?"

We argued about the drowned woman, about whether her death was a suicide or a murder, about whether her appearance that night was an omen or a coincidence, which, you argued, is what an omen is anyway: a coincidence that means something. By the end of summer, even if we were no longer arguing about the woman, we had acquired the habit of arguing about everything else. What was better: dogs or cats, rock or jazz, Cubs or Sox, tacos or egg rolls, right or left, night or day—we could argue about anything.

It no longer required arguing or necking to summon the drowned woman; everywhere we went she surfaced by her own volition: at Rocky's Italian Beef, at Lindo Mexico, at the House of Dong, our favorite Chinese restaurant, a place we still frequented because they had let us sit and talk until late over tiny cups of jasmine tea and broken fortune cookies earlier in the year when it was winter and we had first started going together. We would always kid about going there. "Are you in the mood for Dong, tonight?" I'd ask. It was a dopey joke, and you'd break up at its repeated dopiness. Back then, in winter, if one of us ordered the garlic shrimp, we would both be sure to eat them so that later our mouths tasted the same when we kissed.

Even when she wasn't mentioned, she was there with her drowned body—so dumpy next to yours—and her sad breasts with their wrinkled nipples and sour milk—so saggy beside yours which were still budding—with her swollen belly and her pubic bush colorless in the glare of electric light, with her tangled, slimy hair and her pouting, placid face—so lifeless beside yours—and her skin a pallid white, lightning-flash white, flashbulb white, a whiteness that couldn't be duplicated in daylight—how I'd come to hate that pallor, so cold beside the flush of your skin.

There wasn't a particular night when we finally broke up, just as there wasn't a particular night when we began going together, but I do remember a night in fall when I guessed that it was over. We were parked in the Rambler at the dead end of the street of factories that had been our lovers' lane, listening to a drizzle of rain and dry leaves sprinkle the hood. As always, rain revitalized the smells of the smoked fish and kielbasa in the upholstery. The radio was on too low to hear, the windshield wipers swished at intervals as if we were driving, and the windows were steamed as if we'd been making out. But we'd been arguing as usual, this time about a woman poet who had committed suicide, whose work you were reading. We were sitting, no longer talking or touching, and I remember thinking that I didn't want to argue with you anymore. I didn't want to sit like this in silence; I wanted to talk excitedly all night as we once had, I wanted to find some way that wasn't corny-sounding to tell you how much fun I'd had in your company, how much knowing you had meant to me, and how I had suddenly realized that I'd been so intent on becoming lovers that I'd overlooked how close we'd been as friends. I wanted you to know that. I wanted you to like me again.

"It's sad," I started to say, meaning that I was sorry we had reached a point of sitting silently together, but before I could continue, you challenged the statement.

"What makes you so sure it's sad?"

"What do you mean, what makes me so sure?" I asked, confused by your question, and surprised there could be anything to argue over no matter what you thought I was talking about.

You looked at me as if what was sad was that I would never understand. "For all either one of us know," you said, "she could have been triumphant!"

• •

Maybe when it really ended was that night when I felt we had just reached the beginning, that one time on the beach in the summer between high school and college, when our bodies rammed together so desperately that for a moment I thought we did it, and maybe in our hearts we had, although for me, then, doing it in one's heart didn't quite count. If it did, I supposed we'd all be Casanovas.

I remember riding home together on the El that night, feeling sick and defeated in a way I was embarrassed to mention. Our mute reflections emerged like negative exposures on the dark, greasy window of the train. Lightning branched over the city and when the train entered the subway tunnel, the lights inside flickered as if the power was disrupted although the train continued rocketing beneath the Loop.

When the train emerged again we were on the South Side and it was pouring, a deluge as if the sky had opened to drown the innocent and guilty alike. We hurried from the El station to your house, holding the Navajo blanket over our heads until, soaked, it collapsed. In the dripping doorway of your apartment building, we said goodnight. You were shivering. Your bra showed through the thin blouse plastered to your skin. I swept the wet hair away from your face and kissed you lightly on the lips, then you turned and went inside. I stepped into the rain and you came back out calling after me.

"What?" I asked, feeling a surge of gladness to be summoned back into the doorway with you.

"Want an umbrella?"

I didn't. The downpour was letting up. It felt better to walk back to the El feeling the rain rinse the sand out of my hair, off my legs, until the only places where I could still feel its grit was the crotch of my cutoffs and in each squish of my shoes. A block down the street, I passed a pair of jockey shorts lying in a puddle and realized they were mine, dropped from my back pocket as we ran to your house. I left them behind, wondering if you'd see them and recognize them the next day.

By the time I had climbed the stairs back to the El platform, the rain had stopped. Your scent still hadn't washed from my fingers. The station—the entire city, it seemed—dripped and steamed. The summer sound of crickets and nighthawks echoed from the drenched neighborhood. Alone, I could admit how sick I felt. For you, it was a night that would haunt your dreams. For me, it was another night when I waited, swollen and aching, for what I had secretly nicknamed the Blue Ball Express.

Literally lovesick, groaning inwardly with each lurch of the train and worried that I was damaged for good, I peered out at the passing yellow-lit stations where lonely men stood posted before giant advertisements, pictures of glamorous models defaced by graffiti—the same old scrawled insults and pleas: FUCK YOU, EAT ME. At this late hour the world seemed given over to men without women, men waiting in abject patience for something indeterminate, the way I waited for our next times. I avoided their eyes so that they wouldn't see the pity in mine, pity for them because I'd just been with you, your scent was still on my hands, and there seemed to be so much future ahead.

For me it was another night like that, and by the time I reached my stop I knew I would be feeling better, recovered enough to walk the dark street home making up poems of longing that I never wrote down. I was the D. H. Lawrence of not doing it, the voice of all the would-be lovers who ached and squirmed but still hadn't. From our contortions in doorways, on stairwells, and in the bucket seats of cars we could have composed a *Kama Sutra* of interrupted bliss. It must have been that night when I recalled all the other times of walking home after seeing you so that it seemed as if I was falling into step behind a parade of my former selves—myself walking home on the night we first kissed, myself on the night when I unbuttoned your blouse and kissed your breasts, myself on the night that I lifted your skirt above your thighs and dropped to my knees—each succeeding self another step closer to that irrevocable moment for which our lives seemed poised.

But we didn't, not in the moonlight, or by the phosphorescent lanterns of lightning bugs in your backyard, not beneath the constellations that we couldn't see, let alone decipher, nor in the dark glow that had replaced the real darkness of night, a darkness already stolen from us; not with the skyline rising behind us while the city gradually decayed, not in the heat of summer while a Cold War raged; despite the freedom of youth and the license of first love—because of fate, karma, luck, what does it matter?—we made not doing it a wonder, and yet we didn't, we didn't, we never did.

IN TERMS

Albert Goldbarth

In terms

of math, it would be the divider-line
across a fraction,
it would be the line in one over one, which makes,
of course, a whole—another, greater One. In terms

of myth, however, the condom is something that permits
the bunching muscles of the horse
and the pondering human mind
to coexist; the piper-boy above,
the rat-tat-tat goat hooves below; a woman's
beauty, with the equally beautiful
lilt of a fish. The micron
in between them. I remember a night

of moth—I mean the one that battered
ecstatically at the lamp above our bed,
when we became, ourselves,
two wings and a tiny connection.

CONTRIBUTORS

Kim Addonizio is the author of two poetry collections and co-author, with Dorianne Laux, of *The Poet's Companion: A Guide to the Pleasures of Writing Poetry*. Her fiction has appeared in *Chick-Lit, Chelsea, The Gettysburg Review, Penthouse*, and elsewhere.

Cathryn Alpert is the author of the novel *Rocket City*. Her award-winning short stories have appeared in journals and anthologies including *Best of the West 5, O. Henry Festival Stories, Sudden Fiction (Continued)*, and *Zyzzyva*. She lives in Aptos, California.

Martin Amis is the author of numerous books, including the novels *The Rachel Papers, London Fields, Time's Arrow, The Information*, and *Night Train*. He lives in London.

Cynthia Baughman's stories have appeared in the anthology *Writers Harvest* and in *Quarterly West*. She received her M.F.A. from Cornell University and lives in Douglassville, Pennsylvania, where she is working on a story collection.

Elizabeth Benedict is the author of the novels *Slow Dancing, The Beginner's Book of Dreams, Safe Conduct*, and *The Company of Goodness;* as well as *The Joy of Writing Sex: A Guide for Fiction Writers*.

Michael Benedikt has published five collections of poetry, including *The Badminton at Great Barrington; or, Gustave Mahler & The Chattanooga Choo-Choo* and *The Body*. He has also edited anthologies of poetry and plays and is a former poetry editor of *The Paris Review*. He lives in New York City.

T. Coraghessan Boyle's numerous books include *World's End*, which won the 1988 Pen/Faulkner Award for Best American Fiction; *If the River Was Whiskey; East Is East; The Road to Wellville; Tortilla Curtain;* and *Riven Rock*. He lives outside Santa Barbara and is a professor at the University of Southern California.

Ewing Campbell's novel *Madonna, Maleva* appeared in 1995.

Michelle Chalfoun is the author of *Roustabout*, published in 1996. She lives in Massachusetts with her husband and is at work on a new novel.

Philip Dacey is the author of five books of poetry, as well as many chapbooks, including *The Condom Poems*, *What's Empty Weighs the Most: 24 Sonnets*, and *The Deathbed Playboy*. He teaches at Southwest State University in Marshall, Minnesota.

Denise Duhamel is the author of nine books and chapbooks of poetry, including *Exquisite Politics* (with Maureen Seaton), *Kinky*, and *How the Sky Fell*. Her work has been anthologized in *The Best American Poetry 1994*, *The Best American Poetry 1993*, and *Mondo Barbie*.

Stuart Dybek's poems and stories have appeared in many magazines, including *The Atlantic Monthly*, *The New Yorker*, *Antaeus*, and *Ploughshares*. Three of the stories from his collection *The Coast of Chicago* appeared in O. Henry prize story collections. He lives in Kalamazoo, Michigan and teaches at Western Michigan University.

Martha Elizabeth is a writer and artist in Missoula, Montana. Her poetry collection, *The Return of Pleasure*, won the Montana

Arts Council First Book Award and was published in 1996 by Confluence Press.

Nathan Englander's first story collection, *For the Relief of Unbearable Urges,* will be published by Alfred A. Knopf in 1999. A graduate of the Iowa Writers' Workshop and recipient of a Pushcart Prize in 1997, he lives in Jerusalem.

William Feustle lives in Baldwin, Maryland and writes short stories, novels, and screenplays. He has been published in national and international magazines.

Albert Goldbarth has been publishing notable books of poetry for twenty-five years now; these include *Heaven and Earth* (recipient of the National Book Critics Circle Award), *Adventures in Ancient Egypt,* and *Beyond.* He is also the author of two volumes of essays. He lives in Wichita, Kansas.

John Irving is the author of numerous books, including the novels *The World According to Garp, The Hotel New Hampshire, The Cider House Rules, A Prayer for Owen Meany,* and *Trying to Save Piggy Sneed.*

Hester Kaplan's stories have appeared in *Story, Glimmer Train, Agni Review, Ploughshares, Press,* and other publications. Her story *"Would You Know It Wasn't Love"* appears in *The Best American Short Stories 1998.* She lives in Providence, Rhode Island and is at work on a novel.

Binnie Kirshenbaum is the author of two story collections, *Married Life and Other True Adventures* and *History on a Personal Note,* as well as three novels, *On Mermaid Avenue, A Disturbance in One Place* and *Pure Poetry.* She lives in New York City and teaches at Columbia University.

April Lindner is a Ph.D. candidate in English at the University of Cincinnati. She has also earned degrees from Sarah Lawrence College and the University of New Hampshire. Her poems have appeared in *Prairie Schooner, Peregrine, The Greensboro Review,* and *The Spoon River Quarterly.*

The late **William Matthews'** *Time & Money* won the 1996 National Book Critics Circle Award for poetry. He received the 1997 Ruth Lily Poetry Prize from *Poetry.*

Armistead Maupin is the author of *Maybe the Moon* and the six-volume *Tales of the City* series. He lives in San Francisco.

Andrew McGahan's novel *Praise* was first published in 1992 in Australia after winning the *Australian*/Vogel Literary Award. It also won the Commonwealth Writers' Prize for the Best First Book in the Pacific Region. McGahan's second novel, *1988,* is a prequel to *Praise.*

Anne Rice is the author of eighteen novels. Her first, *Interview with the Vampire,* is one of the bestselling novels of all time. Other books include *The Witching Hour, The Feast of All Saints, Servant of the Bones,* and *Violin.* Her latest book in The Vampire Chronicles, *Pandora,* appeared in 1998. She lives in New Orleans with her husband and son.

James Seay is a recipient of an Award in Literature from the American Academy of Arts and Letters. His most recent book is *Open Field, Understory: New and Selected Poems.* He teaches creative writing at the University of North Carolina, Chapel Hill.

Gregg Shapiro's poetry and fiction have been published in magazines and anthologies including *Gargoyle, Christopher Street, Mondo Barbie, Unsettling America,* and *Mondo Marilyn.* He lives in Chicago.

Alison Stone's poems have appeared in *Poetry*, *The Paris Review*, *Ploughshares*, and other magazines and anthologies. She has been awarded *NY Quarterly's* Madeline Sadin Award and *Poetry's* Frederick Boer Prize. She is a psychotherapist in private practice in New York City.

Chase Twichell's most recent book is *Ghost of Eden*. She teaches creative writing at Princeton University and Goddard College.

Ronald Wallace is the author of nine books of poetry and criticism, including *Time's Fancy*, *The Makings of Happiness*, and *God Be with the Clown: Humor in American Poetry*. He is director of creative writing at the University of Wisconsin, Madison, and poetry editor for the University of Wisconsin Press.

CREDITS

"A Brief History of Condoms" copyright © 1997 Kim Addonizio

"Condomology in Twelve Easy Lessons" copyright © 1997 by Cathryn Alpert

"Eleven ten: The Rachel Papers, volume two," from *The Rachel Papers* by Martin Amis. Copyright © 1988 by Martin Amis. Reprinted by permission of Harmony Books, a division of Crown Publishers, Inc.

"Safety Speech" appeared in *Writers Harvest* (Harcourt Brace). Copyright © 1994 Cynthia Baughman.

"Joy" copyright © 1997 Elizabeth Benedict

"All That Talk About 'High-Tech' in the Future Notwithstanding, Why the 21st Century Might Well Turn Out to Be Full of a Whole Lot of Clumsy People!" copyright © 1995 by Michael Benedikt. First published in *The New Republic*, July 17-24, 1995. Reprinted by permission of the author.

"Modern Love", from *If the River Was Whiskey* by T. Coraghessan Boyle. Copyright © 1989 by T. Coraghessan Boyle. Used by permission of Viking Penguin, a division of Penguin Books USA Inc.

"Conveniences" was first published in *The Kenyon Review*. Copyright © 1989 Ewing Campbell

CREDITS

ABOUT THE EDITORS

Mitch Roberson is studying poetry in the Master of Fine Arts program at Vermont College. He lives with his wife in Jersey City, New Jersey.

Julia Dubner has a Master of Arts in fiction writing from the University of California at Davis. She works in publishing in New York City, and lives with her husband in Jersey City, New Jersey.